Tread Softly

by CORINNE GERSON

Cover illustration
by Lydia Rosier

This book is being published simultaneously in hardcover and paperback editions. The hardcover edition is available through Atheneum Publishers, a division of the Macmillan Publishing Co., Inc., 866 Third Avenue, New York, N.Y. 10022.

SCHOLASTIC BOOK SERVICES

NEW YORK • TORONTO • LONDON • AUCKLAND • SYDNEY • TOKYO

ISBN 0-590-31904-3

12 11 10 9 8 7 6 5 4 3 2 1   4   1 2 3 4 5 6/8

Printed in the U.S.A.   06

TO MOTHER
who always trod softly on my dreams

AND TO EVERETT
who helped me live them

1

When I went into Mayo's to buy a pack of gum, the whole big place was empty except for this pretty woman and her little boy. I was so fascinated watching them that I pretended I came in for a comic book and couldn't decide which one to buy. That's stupid to begin with, because I don't even read comic books — I always thought they were pretty silly. But the people who work at Mayo's don't know that, so I just browsed and watched the little boy who was examining the stuffed animals next to the candy counter. He looked like one of those little kids in picture books with round faces and big blue eyes. But the nicest thing about it all was the way the woman — I guessed she was his mother, though she looked awfully young — the way she was looking at him. I mean, like he was the most wonderful thing in the world to watch. He was, but he was her own son — I soon found that out — and she was watching him with so much *enjoyment*. She let him examine every single animal as long as he wanted to, until he picked out the one he liked best. And then changed his mind three times. I kept stealing side glances at them, making believe I was looking at the magazines. She was very pretty, with beautiful slanted eyes that were the same golden color, almost, as her hair. She was wearing a summer dress and open sandals, and her hair was pulled back with a green silk scarf.

The little boy finally picked out a fat blue pig, and while she was paying for it, he dropped it right on my foot. I picked it up and just stared at it like it was the greatest thing I ever saw, and started saying things like, "Oh, Mr. Pig, you must be lost!" You know, baby things like that that little kids think are funny. And wow, this little kid sure did.

"It's mine. *My* piggy!" he screamed up at

me, reaching for the pig and giggling away. That was when his mother noticed me.

"Say thank you to the nice girl for picking up your toy, Tommy."

Tommy. If I had a little brother I'd want his name to be Tommy.

"Thank you," Tommy burbled, and his mother smiled.

"I wish I could get my little sister to say thank you." The words just slipped out before I could stop them. Because I don't really have a little sister. But I just couldn't help saying it — I wanted to talk to the woman, and besides, she'd never know the difference.

"How old is your little sister?" she asked me, putting her change in her wallet.

"Almost three. Her name is Gaby."

"And how old are you?"

"I'll be twelve in August," I told her. "I'm going into junior high."

"You seem to really care about little kids," she said, taking Tommy's hand. "Your sister is lucky."

I dropped my eyes and mumbled, "Thank you." I was beginning to feel embarrassed, but in a way I wished she'd stay and talk to me. She was so nice. I got my wish.

"Your mother's lucky, too. You must be a tremendous help to her with your little sister."

"Oh, I do lots for Gaby — taking her places and reading to her. But — well, Mums says she doesn't want me always sticking around the house this summer, so I decided to look for a job." I didn't know anything like this was going to come out, though I had been thinking of it. And somehow, when I saw her and the way she watched her little boy, I thought of the nice life she must lead.

"A job? You mean — baby-sitting?"

"Yes — like that. You know, mother's helper. I'm very good at it."

"I'll bet you are. By the way, I'm Vera Folsom. What's your name, hon?"

Hon. Something warm wrapped around me. "Carol Ann Tate." I smiled my brightest. "Everyone calls me Kitten."

"Well" — she stared at me hard and then smiled slowly — "maybe we can make a deal, Kitten. Why, you do look like a kitten! With those beautiful green eyes and all those freckles! Look, Kitten, do you like being with little children? I mean *really* like being with them? Do you have lots of patience to play with them and things?"

"Oh, yes, I love to! I make up all kinds of

silly games with Gaby, and Mums tells me if I keep it up I'll be a nursery-school teacher or something."

"Look, are you really serious about a job — Carol Ann, that's a pretty name, too. Does everyone really call you Kitten?"

I nodded. "My initials spell CAT. That's how it started." She smiled, so I was glad I'd said it, even though it wasn't true. It's what I tell people when they ask me how I got the nickname, but it really started when I was a baby and my parents called me Pussycat. But that was in what I think of as my First Life. That stopped when The Tragedy happened and my brother, Peter, and I went to live with my grandmother and grandfather. I added quickly, "Yes, I really am looking for a job. Do you know anyone who needs a mother's helper for the summer?"

She nodded decidedly. "I sure do, Kitten. Me. If it's all right with your parents, Tommy and I would love to have you start tomorrow."

"Oh, sure, that'll be okay. I told them I was going to look for a job and they said fine."

"How does forty dollars a week seem?"

"That would be great," I said, trying to sound businesslike.

She took a little pad and pen from her handbag and wrote on it. "Here, this is our address. Come by around nine, all right?"

I squeezed the folded piece of paper so hard I almost couldn't open it without tearing it when I got home. A job — a real job! I couldn't believe it! One minute I was buying a pack of gum and the next I had a job for the whole summer making more money than I'd ever earned before. And I hadn't even gone out looking for it, not really.

"Grandma, you'll never guess what happened to me!"

She bustled over to me, her face getting all wrinkled with worry. "What happened, Kitten?"

"No, it's something good." I threw my arms around her. Grandma is big and wide, so I just hung on and said, "I got a job. For the whole summer!"

"A job! What on earth doing, dear?"

"Being a mother's helper to this real nice lady and her little boy, Tommy. He's three, Grandma, and he's adorable. Like one of those pictures in magazines."

Grandma took hold of my hands and smiled down at me. "Well, now, isn't that nice! But how in the world did it ever happen, dear?"

I told her about it, all except the part I made

6

up about my Family, and she shook her head. "Well, it's true, Kitten, fortune favors the bold."

I turned away because I didn't want her to see me wrinkle my nose. I knew it had to come soon — one of her sayings — and whenever it did I couldn't help making a face. Grandpa and Grandma had a saying for everything — but everything. And if they didn't have a saying, they had a poem, or part of one. Sometimes Peter and I would think up a subject and then bring it into our regular conversation to see if they had a saying for it — something kooky, to try to stump them. But we never could.

"Well," I said now, "I guess I was a little bold, but it was worth it. Oh, Grandma, it's going to be so much fun!"

She patted my head, smiling. "Faith is the antiseptic of the soul."

There was a loud bang and we both jumped. Peter the Pest, standing in the doorway, had just dropped his tackle box, and a little pool started forming around him and the box. His clothes were all stuck to him and he looked like a shipwreck victim.

"I didn't catch a single thing the whole day, and then I fell in the lake!" he moaned.

"Well, young man," Grandma began, shaking her head, "you can march yourself right up into the bathtub."

"The bathtub! You gotta be kidding! I'm sopping wet! If I have to get into any more water, I'll melt and flow down the drain."

He sounded so upset — I burst out laughing, and he glared at me angrily. *"You!* One of these day *you'll* see." Then he spun around to Grandma. "It's always *me!*" he half sobbed. "You never make *her* take a bath. I don't know when she took a bath last. Just because she's a girl — probably under all those pretty clothes there's ten layers of dirt!"

I wasn't laughing anymore and was just working up some steam for a good fight when he suddenly burst into tears and ran out of the room. Suddenly I felt awfully sorry for him. After all, he was only two years old when our parents died and probably couldn't even remember them. And he didn't have the extra family I did, I was sure of that. He just had his friends Skint and Charlie and his fishing, and Grandma making him take baths all the time, and Grandpa too old and tired to play ball with him and do the other things boys' fathers did with them. And he had me, who didn't get yelled at very much and I guess always seemed to have it easier and maybe better. I figured then that life wasn't so easy for Peter. It wasn't, as Grandma and Grandpa would say, a bowl of cherries.

"Home is the wanderer," I heard later as I was setting the table. The kitchen screen door thudded gently. "Home from the hill." Grandpa set down his lunch pail and gave me a soft pat on the shoulder, and I stood on tiptoes to give him his hello kiss. Before I could get the words out, Grandma said, "Kitten found herself a job today, Thomas. A mother's helper to a nice lady with a cute little boy. Isn't that nice?"

"Well, well, how did you go and do something like that, Kitten?" When I told him the story he shook his head. " 'Ability will see a chance and snatch it. Who has a match will find a place to scratch it.' You certainly know what you're about, little Kitten, don't you?"

"What did Kitten do?"

Everyone turned to see Peter standing in the doorway, his yellow terry robe wrapped around him and his hair plastered down on his head.

"I got a job, Peter, taking care of this little boy for the whole summer. Maybe you can come over sometime and play with him."

"Are you crazy? What would I want to play with a little kid for?"

I shrugged. "Well, if you don't have anything to do one day. And maybe sometime we could take him fishing. You could show him — "

"Well, I'll see," he muttered. "If I have some time, maybe. But I'm pretty busy, you know."

"Now come," Grandma called from the kitchen, "let's have our supper before it gets cold."

After Peter and I finished the dishes, I went over to my best friend Jeannie's. She lives three houses away, and Ann lives around the corner on the next block. Actually the three of us were best friends — we hardly did anything without each other. Except for the special things that Jeannie's and Ann's families did together, because their parents were friends, too. I often thought if my mother and father hadn't died they would probably be Jeannie's and Ann's parents' friends, and then I'd get to go on those family things, too, and even Peter. I guess the reason they never asked me now was because Grandma and Grandpa couldn't reciprocate.

"I have something special to tell you," I said when Jeannie came to the door. "But first let's go get Ann, because I want to tell you both at the same time."

"She's here already," Jeannie said, grabbing my hand and dragging me into the TV room. Ann was lying on the floor, her head resting in her cupped hands, watching a perfume commercial, and Jeannie's two little brothers were rolling around her play-fighting. "Ann, Kitten has something special to tell us."

"Oh, hi, Kitten. Something good?"

"Something wonderful," I said. "I got a job — for the whole summer!"

They both gasped, really gasped. "Honest?" Ann said, and Jeannie squealed, "What kind of a job?"

When I told them, their faces sort of sagged. "Hey, gee, that's nice, Kitten," Ann said, and Jeannie mumbled, "Yeah, great." But I could tell they didn't really think so. I remembered how excited we all were that winter when we got our first baby-sitting jobs. They were daytime jobs, after school and on weekends, and only for an hour or two. But by the time school was over, Jeannie and Ann were getting bored with it, because they both had little brothers and sisters they had to take care of, so it wasn't as much fun for them. Besides they got big allowances from their parents and didn't really need the money.

"Anyway," I went on, "I'm starting tomorrow, and Mrs. Folsom said — "

"Hey, wait," Jeannie cut in, "did you say Mrs. Folsom? Is her little boy's name Tommy?"

"Yes. Do you know her?"

"Is her husband a doctor?"

I shrugged. "I don't know. But they live on Willow Avenue."

Jeannie snapped her fingers. "That's the one. My cousin Donna used to baby-sit for them! She's real pretty, Mrs. Folsom? And they have this gorgeous house — "

"Yes, she is real pretty! I haven't seen their house yet, but it must be the same people. Tommy's three."

"Oh, yes, I was there with her once. Wow, wait till you see that place. Is it ever something!"

"That's funny," Ann said now. "Why doesn't Donna sit for them anymore?"

"Mrs. Folsom wanted her to, but she got a job in a day camp this summer. Anyway I don't think she'd want to work there now."

My heart started beating a little faster, the

way it did when I started hearing things I didn't really want to.

"Why not?" Ann asked.

Jeannie shrugged, looking at me strangely. "Oh, I don't know exactly. She always said Mrs. Folsom is sort of — funny."

"What do you mean?" I asked.

"Well, I guess — I don't know, but she's like one of those real phony people that acts nice to you, but you don't know what she's really thinking." Jeannie giggled. "Donna said she's a busybody, but she says that about everyone."

"Oh, don't pay any attention, Kitten!" Ann said then. "I'm sure you're going to like it, especially if the little boy is so cute."

"He's adorable!" Jeannie said. "I only saw him that once, but he was so smart, too. And he had so many toys! Donna said he's spoiled."

I knew Donna and I'd always liked her. I didn't think she'd say things about people that weren't true. But then I knew that you can't always go by others' feelings about people either. After all there were kids I liked that my friends didn't. One of Grandma's favorites came to me then: "Judge not that ye be not judged." Sayings like that came in handy sometimes. I wasn't even going to think about how Donna felt anymore. I was going to start my new job feeling just as happy as I was before I told Jeannie and Ann about it.

"You see," I explained to Mums after I got into bed that night, "I know they're my best friends and all, but sometimes I feel so left out." Mums was the only one I could talk to like that. Mums was my make-believe mother. Mums and Daddy and Buck, my teen-age brother, and Gaby — short for Gabrielle — my little sister. That was my whole make-believe family. I made them up when I was five, the year after my real mother and father died in a car accident. Every night when I went to bed I would climb into my other world with my make-believe family, and it made me feel good. If I had a problem, I'd talk about it with Mums. She was young and pretty, like Mrs. Folsom, and Daddy always called me his princess, and Buck would ruffle my hair and kid me about what a knockout I was going to be in a few years, and Gaby would always follow me around and want me to teach her things. I knew it wasn't real and that it was only for special times, like before I went to sleep at night or sometimes when I woke up in the morning or just quiet times during the day when I was feeling a little lonely.

This night I needed to talk to Mums. I started out with what Jeannie had said about Mrs. Folsom and then told what happened later when Ann asked Jeannie what she was going to wear to the picnic Sunday. Jeannie gave her this look and Ann got all flustered. Then they both tried to cover up, and I was so embarrassed I could have died. I knew the two families were going together, the way they did, and that there were plenty of their own kids, but I was just one more and I could have even brought my own food. I went home right after that and I went to bed real early because I had to have a long visit with my Family. I told Grandma and Grandpa I was tired and had to get up early to be at my job, and they smiled and kissed me and gave me the old one-two about "Early to bed, early to rise, makes a girl healthy, wealthy, and wise," and I laughed and said, "Yeah, well, I'm pretty healthy and I guess I'm getting wise and I sure *hope* I'll get wealthy." Then I ran upstairs real fast so they wouldn't hit me with another one about greed or something even more awful.

Mums cuddled me against her when I told her about Jeannie and Ann, and when I started crying she kissed me and said, "Don't you worry, Kitten darling, you're going to have such a wonderful summer you won't even have time to think about Jeannie and Ann. You're growing up and you have all kinds of exciting things in store for you."

Then I told her about my other problem — my *real* problem — about how I had lied to Mrs. Folsom about my family. "I didn't really mean to, it just slipped out. It's the first time in my life that ever happened."

Mums had that understanding smile. It was the same smile that I remembered my real mother had. She put both her hands on my shoulders and said, "Look, darling, it's very simple. You'll just tell her the truth. Yes, now listen to me. You'll explain about what happened to you when you were four, and that you made up this *game*. You never really told anyone about it before, but it's just something that makes you feel good, and it slipped out when you were talking with her because you felt so comfortable being around her. She's such a nice lady, Kitten, she'll understand that it wasn't really a lie."

"Are you sure?" I said, and she nodded her head solemnly.

"Yes, Kitten, I'm sure."

And then I fell asleep.

2

"Good morning, Kitten. You're very prompt!" Mrs. Folsom, standing in her doorway, looked like a fashion model in her pink shirt and white jeans and sandals. "Come in, dear."

I had never been inside a house like the Folsoms' before — one of those real modern split-level kind, with beautiful wood on the outside and all fancy bushes and trees and the kind of lawn that's so perfect it looks fake. When I followed her into the entrance hall, I tried not to stare, but my eyes felt like bullets shooting around from the shiny white vinyl floor with its huge black design to the fancy modern black-and-gold chandelier that came way down low.

"Kitten, Kitten!" Tommy screeched, bounding in and throwing his arms around my legs so hard I almost fell over. I bent down and picked him up and whirled him around, and he shrieked, "More, more!"

"Whoa, wait!" Mrs. Folsom was laughing, but she put out her arms and took Tommy. "Let this poor girl catch her breath, darling. There'll be all day to play."

I smiled up at him. He was absolutely the cutest little kid I had ever seen in my life. I hugged myself inside with my own happiness.

Mrs. Folsom set Tommy down. "Come, let's show Kitten around our house," she said.

I'll never forget that tour. It's funny, but sometimes you get real used to things that seemed so strange at the beginning and you don't think about it very much, but you always remember the first time you saw them and the way you felt. That's the way it was with that house. It was like a dream house. There were two great big rooms on the entrance floor. One was Mrs. Folsom's studio. She was a painter, and it was filled with paintings stacked up on the floor and an easel and a sink and cabinets and all the junk painters use. And one whole wall was glass! Outside of it were grass and trees and way back a big metal fence.

"Tommy went to play group every morning. It just closed for the summer. That's when I paint," she was saying while I tried not to let my mouth hang open in shock at all this unbelievable stuff I was seeing. "After you get here, you can straighten up the kitchen from breakfast and then tidy up Tommy's room."

"Can I help?" Tommy cried.

"Yes, of course," she said, ruffling his hair. "The rest of the morning is playtime. Claire comes in every afternoon to clean and do laundry, but by then lunch is over and Tommy is in for his nap, and you'll have free time to rest. With this little monster you'll need it!"

Tommy grabbed my hand and squeezed it. "I'm a monster!" he repeated, and we all laughed.

By now we were in the next room, even bigger than the studio. It was a playroom, with a bar on one side and low couches and chairs and shelves with a TV and stereo and big cupboards that Tommy flung open to show me his collection of toys and games. And in this room, too, one whole wall was glass. "Is that the next-door neighbor's fence?" I asked, pointing outside.

"Oh, no, that's the fence around our pool area," Mrs. Folsom said.

"Your pool? You mean a swimming pool?"

Mrs. Folsom laughed. I must have looked pretty funny. "Oh, didn't I tell you we have one? I'm sorry, Kitten. Tommy loves the pool, and there's no reason why you can't go in every afternoon that's nice. Do you like swimming?"

"I love it! I'm going to go out for Junior Lifesaver next year."

"Marvelous! I never even thought to ask you. Today all the kids can swim." She went over to the glass wall that turned out to be sliding doors and pushed them open. "Let's go down and show you the pool."

Now it was really like a movie. It was an honest-to-goodness swimming pool, with a pretty, curvy shape, a diving board, and everything! She made sure to show me the shallow end with the steps and where Tommy was to stay, and I tried to listen carefully, but it sure was hard when there were so many things to look at. There were all these beautiful lounge chairs and tables with umbrellas. I'd never seen anything like it — wait till I told Jeannie and Ann about this! And my Family, too. That reminded me of what I had to tell Mrs. Folsom.

But she kept up this running conversation, like a tour guide, and I was so knocked out by the rest of the house that I could hardly talk myself. The kitchen on the middle floor was straight out of a magazine with a butcher-block counter in the center and a refrigerator that gave ice water like from a water fountain. The living room had a grand piano and carpeting so thick it felt like you were walking around on foam-rubber mattresses. But about the best of all was Tommy's room.

The first thing I thought of when I saw it was how much Peter would have loved a room like that. It had bunk beds, and Peter always said if he was born again, he'd want to come back as a kid who slept on the top of a bunk bed. And there were all kinds of toys, a big rocking horse and a little jungle gym in one corner, and this red-white-and-blue rug in the shape of a toy soldier, with curtains that had the same design. There were stuffed animals all over the place, of every size and style and color, and Tommy just about went crazy showing me every single thing in the room. I never saw so many beautiful toys in my life, and I was thinking how I wouldn't mind playing with some of them myself.

"I guess you're pretty used to all this," Mrs.

Folsom was saying, "having a little sister yourself."

It was like putting a cold knife across my forehead, the way Grandma did when I bumped myself to keep it from getting black and blue.

"Uh, there's something I want to talk to you about, Mrs. Folsom." At last the time had come.

"Kitten, is it something that we can wait to chat over at lunch?" She was looking at her watch. "I'm way behind, and I'd really like to get some painting in this morning. I'll just give you the schedule for today, and we can sit and talk later when we can relax. Is that all right with you, hon?" She gave me that glowing smile, and I just nodded dumbly. "Oh — unless it's something urgent?"

"No, no, it can wait." *Chicken chicken chicken!* a voice inside me screamed. *Don't let the chance go by!*

But I did. I just couldn't help it. There was no way I could bring up the subject then, though. Not when she was in such a hurry. Not then or for the rest of the day, even though I promised myself I wasn't going to leave that house without getting everything all straightened out. That was the first promise I broke to myself.

I really tried, though. After I got Tommy's room tidied, Mrs. Folsom called me into her studio. "How do you like it, Kitten?" she said, pointing at the canvas she was working on.

"Why, that's Tommy! Oh, Mrs. Folsom, it's wonderful! You're really *good*!"

Her eyes were sparkling and her face got a little pink. Sitting there like that in her smudged-up smock, she looked like a little kid. I felt happy just watching her.

"I'm hungry!" Tommy suddenly yelled. "Can I have a peanut butter sandwich?"

Mrs. Folsom glanced at her watch. "Heavens, I didn't dream it was this late. Kitten, why don't you fix him one and take whatever you want for yourself from the fridge — there's lots of stuff, just poke around."

"All right. Would you like me to fix something for you, Mrs. Folsom?"

"Thank you, hon, it's all right. I'll just have some cottage cheese and fruit. I have a tennis date in an hour, so I've got to move."

Tommy was guzzling his chocolate milk by the time she came into the kitchen, and I had already eaten. She had changed into a tennis dress, one with a pink embroidered pocket and pink lace edging all around. Little pink pom-poms popped out from behind her sneakers. "Kitten, I really got off the track today," she said, moving around the kitchen as she got herself a plate of cottage cheese and slices of peaches and pears. "You'll have to forgive me." She began eating quickly and taking long gulps of diet soda. "I'm usually a very organized person and schedule my time pretty well. But today being your first day and having to show you everything, time just got away from me. Look, hon, I really ought to give you instructions for the rest of the day, since I'll be gone all afternoon. Then we can talk. Now look at Tommy, his eyes are starting to close already. He can just about make it from lunch to his nap. Sometimes his head goes right down on the table, and you have to carry him up to his bed."

Tommy shook his head groggily. "No, I don't need a nap. I'm not tired today." His eyelids fluttered, and Mrs. Folsom and I exchanged secret smiles.

"Never mind, my little sweetheart. Look, why don't you take Kitten up to your room and show her your animals?" She winked at me, and it made me feel so important, like I was her conspirator.

He climbed off his stool and giving a big yawn said, "Come, see my animals."

I went off after him, and Mrs. Folsom followed us up, motioning for me to put him into his bed. His eyes were just closing as I laid him down, and he reached out for the big teddy bear Mrs. Folsom handed over. We both tiptoed out of the room, and she quietly closed his door, whispering, "He'll be out for a good hour and a half, maybe even longer. I've got just enough time for a cup of coffee." She led the way back to the kitchen. "I'll give you instructions for the rest of the day, and then we can have our talk before I leave."

My heart started pounding. I hoped I'd remember the things I had been rehearsing the night before, the way I was going to explain it so she would understand and just laugh it off, like Mums was so sure she would. I could hardly keep my mind on what she was telling me — how when Tommy got up from his nap I should get him into his bathing suit and all. "Oh, how silly of me!" she cried suddenly. "I never even told you to bring your suit or anything. But wait — how far away do you live, Kitten?"

"About eight blocks."

"Oh, that's not so bad. Would you feel like

going home for your swimming things after Claire comes? There won't be any problem — you don't even have to come back right away, as long as you're here when Tommy gets up. Claire will be around for him. It's a lovely day for the pool."

"Sure, that's a good idea."

There was a clicking sound at the front door, and Mrs. Folsom said, "Well, what do you know — there's Claire. We're in here, Claire," she called.

I was pretty surprised when a black woman about as old as Grandma walked into the kitchen. But unlike Grandma she was small and real thin. I guess because of the way Mrs. Folsom had talked about Claire I just thought that she would be some real young woman, younger even than Mrs. Folsom, and when she said, "Claire, this is my mother's helper, Kitten. Kitten, this is Claire," I just smiled and said, "How do you do," but there was a lump in my throat because I didn't know how I was going to call this old lady by her first name.

She looked at me and pursed her lips. "Well, Kitten, eh?" Then she gave Mrs. Folsom a big smile. "So now you've gone and got yourself a pussycat!" I liked Claire. She was real nice and friendly. She and Mrs. Folsom got into a conversation about the laundry and Dr. Folsom's shirts. A doctor! No wonder they were so rich! I wondered if I would ever meet him.

I looked at the clock. It was almost time for Mrs. Folsom to go, and I was wishing Claire would leave so I could have my talk. All of a sudden Mrs. Folsom turned to me. "Oh, Kitten, you wanted to talk to me about something."

Claire started picking up the dirty dishes, and I looked around for a private place where she wouldn't be able to hear. After all it was going to be hard enough to tell Mrs. Folsom about how I'd made up this whole story about myself. I sure didn't want somebody else listening in, too. "It's okay, Mrs. Folsom, I don't want you to be late for your appointment."

She glanced over at Claire. "Oh, yes. Well, look, hon, I expect to be home before you leave. Then we can sit around and have a nice talk. You'll probably have a lot more questions by then anyway, so you might as well save them all up."

That's what she thought was on my mind, just some questions. Probably about Tommy and what she expected of me each day. Funny, I thought then, I hadn't even wondered about that. There didn't seem to be time to.

"A swimming pool!" Grandma exclaimed when I told her about it after I got home. "My, my, my!" She thought for a moment and I braced myself. Would it be a new one? "Riches," she said slowly, "are not from an abundance of worldly goods, but from a contented mind."

I smiled. That was a pretty good one. When I was younger I often used to think that Grandma and Grandpa ought to sit down and make a list of all their sayings and number them. Then they could have private conversations just by using numbers, and no one else would know what they were talking about. Can you just see them? Grandma saying, "Thirty-two," and Grandpa nodding as he'd reply, "Yes, how true." But then there were some good sayings that I wouldn't want to miss. And it was kind of fun waiting each time to see if they were going to come up with a new one. It was amazing how often they did.

When I told Grandma Mrs. Folsom's husband was a doctor, she was pretty impressed, too. We looked through my things and packed a little bag with my suit and thongs and terry cape, and Grandma said she would make me another cape. She looked happy when I waved good-bye. I was glad to be going back to the

Folsoms', because the house and the whole street were awfully quiet. Peter was off fishing, and Jeannie and Ann were probably doing something together, but it couldn't have been as much fun as what I was doing.

The afternoon got awfully hot and Tommy couldn't wait to get into the pool. He had about as many water toys as he had regular stuff, and it wasn't easy keeping track of them and him in the water. But it was fun, and I felt like a really important person being in that beautiful place with an adorable little kid who wanted my attention every single minute. By the time Mrs. Folsom got home, we had just changed out of our wet things and I was rubbing Tommy's curls with a towel on the lawn right outside the playroom.

"Well, Kitten, how was your day?" She swept Tommy up and started tickling and kissing him, and he screamed with laughter. I wasn't going to mind telling her my story in front of Tommy — he wouldn't know what it was all about anyway, and besides the three of us would soon be like a family. I quickly told her about the whole afternoon, and Tommy kept interrupting to repeat my words, as if he was telling the story and I was helping him. Mrs. Folsom and I smiled about it, and I wished it would go on forever so I wouldn't have to get to the awful part. But I pushed myself along. "Mrs. Folsom, what I wanted to tell you — "

"Mrs. Folsom, excuse me." Claire had appeared from inside. "Telephone call for you — your sister, from California."

Mrs. Folsom gasped. "Oh, I wonder if Cliff got that directorship!" She started inside, then suddenly turned to me. "Kitten, I'm going to be a while. Why don't you run along. You've had a long day. We'll talk first thing in the morning, okay?"

Before I could even answer, she was gone. Claire stood there smiling at me. "This lady doesn't have a minute for an extra breath, not if she doesn't make an appointment for it beforehand. Now look, honey, why don't you leave your swimming things here. I'll have them ready for you nice when you come tomorrow."

"Oh, thank you. Thank you very much!"

I was off the hook till tomorrow.

But, like I'm sure Grandma would have said, tomorrow never came. It's hard to believe, but I never found the chance to tell Mrs. Folsom how I had made up that story about my family. Every time I worked myself up to it, there was another interruption, just like the first day. The truth is Mrs. Folsom didn't really seem interested in talking about things like that anyway, and then the time went on and it got less and less important to me, too. Oh, she talked to me a lot, and I talked to her, too. But it was never personal stuff about me. Her life was so busy and so interesting that nothing else seemed to matter. She loved talking about Tommy and the things he did and what we did together when she was away, which was about every afternoon, unless she had company. In that way she was really interested in me, and I realized that's all that was important anyway. By the time a couple of weeks went by, I was sure she had forgotten about the whole thing. She had never even mentioned my little sister again, except when she had introduced me to Dr. Folsom.

He took Wednesdays off and usually played golf, and sometimes she went along, too, but they always went out afterward. Claire would stay on then to take care of Tommy till they came home.

"Darling, this is Kitten," she had said when I came that first Wednesday. He was wearing a fancy kind of T-shirt and white slacks and sneakers. He was tall and had curly reddish hair and was he ever handsome! He didn't look anything like a doctor.

"Well, it's very nice to meet you at last, Kitten." He had such a nice smile. Even his eyes were smiling at me. "Tommy's been talking about you so much, and my wife, too."

"Oh." I smiled back, but I couldn't think of anything else to say.

He was looking at me very hard now — almost as if he was examining me.

"I understand you're twelve?" he said.

"Almost," I answered. "I'll be twelve August second."

His eyebrows rose and he glanced over at his wife.

"She's got a little sister exactly Tommy's age," she said quickly. "And she's helped take care of her since she was born. Didn't you, Kitten?"

I nodded, feeling numb. It was almost as if Mrs. Folsom was on trial for me being old enough and good enough to take care of their little boy.

"No, no, it's all a mistake!" I wanted to scream. "I've been meaning to tell you ever since that first day, but I never had the chance." But, of course, I couldn't. Certainly not now.

I was just nodding dumbly to Mrs. Folsom's question, but Dr. Folsom gave me a nice smile now as he said, "Well, no wonder you're a real pro. Being around a child that way is the best kind of experience you can get. I know you'll do a fine job with Tommy this summer. I just wanted to be sure you're a responsible young lady, which my wife assures me you are." Now he turned to Mrs. Folsom. "Look, Vera, I want to get an early start today. Why don't you and Paula meet us at the club for lunch?"

Their voices droned on as I turned away. That was a close call. There was no way I was going to be able to tell Mrs. Folsom the truth about my Family now, not with Dr. Folsom having such strict rules. I just hoped the subject would never come up again. I gave that part of my life, the make-believe part, a shove back to where it belonged and promised myself to keep my big mouth shut from now on.

Little by little the real part of my life — going to the Folsoms' every day and being a part of their world — started being all that mattered anymore. Especially when Mrs. Folsom asked if she could paint me. It was the end of my second week there, after she finished Tommy's portrait.

"I want to try something new, Kitten, and

you have the perfect face for it. You'd only have to sit for me for a couple of weeks, and Tommy can play around us while we work."

While we work. I never did such nice work in my whole life! I would sit in her beautiful, sunny studio and she would paint away and we would talk. We set up an easel for Tommy, and he painted his own pictures and played with his modeling clay all during that time. Mrs. Folsom would tell me about the things that she did with her friends and the places she traveled to with her husband, and in a way it was like a visit between two grown-ups. She often asked me how I liked the way she was wearing her hair or which of her outfits looked nicer, and things like that. She didn't ask me anything about myself, and I was glad, because my life was just so ordinary. And I didn't want to have any more problems about my make-believe life, so it was better that she liked talking about herself with me. She even told me about her childhood. She said she was very poor as a little girl, that she only ever had one toy — a doll.

"I guess that's why Tommy has so much," she said with a sort of embarrassed laugh. "I know we spoil him, but sometimes you can't help some things you do." That was the first time I remembered what Jeannie had told me about the way her cousin Donna felt about Mrs. Folsom. It upset me that people could get such wrong impressions.

I would do the tidying up during Tommy's nap, and whatever I didn't finish Claire would do. The weather was gorgeous, and Tommy and I went into the pool practically every day. By the time I'd get home each day, I was really beat. And really happy. Sometimes I'd go over to Jeannie's and Ann's after supper, and they would tell me about the boring things they'd done, and then I would tell them about my day. I honestly think that sometimes they didn't believe me, the looks I'd see them sneaking at each other. Like when Mrs. Folsom would have these fancy splash parties. She would have a luncheon during Tommy's nap-time, and Claire and I would set up and serve. By the time Tommy was up from his nap, the women would leave the pool and go in the playroom for drinks, and then Tommy and I would go swimming. Sometimes Mrs. Folsom and her friends would come back out and play around in the pool with Tommy, and I'd have time to swim around by myself or just lie back on one of the lounges and bake in the sun for a while without having to jump up every minute to watch Tommy, and that was absolute heaven. That's why I was so crazy about it when Mrs. Folsom had her parties. Besides, it was fun helping serve. I loved looking at all the pretty women and their beautiful outfits, and they would always say real nice things to me. Other times Mrs. Folsom would go to her friends' or play tennis, and then Tommy and I would just follow our old routine.

But I never got tired of it, never once. He was so active and so clever I never had time to sit and be bored. And he was so affectionate and lovable that taking care of him was always fun. It's true, he was a little spoiled. Claire would shake her head and say he was so spoiled it was a wonder he was so sweet, and we would just shrug and smile. I didn't even mind the tantrums he had, because they wouldn't last long, and I knew you had to expect that from little kids. I remembered Peter's tantrums, and how Grandma and Grandpa used to try to talk him out of them with their sayings, and how all I ever wanted to do was sock him. But now that I was older I realized how much patience you had to have with little kids and how smart Grandma and Grandpa had been with us. I learned a lot of things like that from my job, and it was so nice and so different from anything I'd ever done in my life before. But the one part that stayed exactly the same was the visits with my Family. Especially at night, when I had so many wonderful things to tell them.

3

It took Mrs. Folsom two weeks to do my portrait. I couldn't believe it when I saw it. It didn't look anything like me. In fact it didn't look anything like a person. Not until you squinched up your eyes and tilted your head. Then somehow the painting *did* look like me! My face was all little blocks of different colors, and the background had lots of other queer shapes. The more I saw it, the more fascinated I became. Mrs. Folsom was crazy about it. She said it was her first try at abstract expressionism, whatever that was, and had turned out better than she dreamed it would. She kept it around in her studio the whole

39

summer, and one time some people came over to see her work and wanted to buy some paintings.

I couldn't help overhearing, because Tommy and I were in the playroom right next to the studio, and Tommy was all wrapped up in building a tower with big blocks. I heard them asking about my painting and another one that was supposed to be a vase of flowers, but looked to me more like the finger paintings Peter used to do in kindergarten. But Mrs. Folsom told them no, that she had promised to show some of her work in the August outdoor art show, and these were two she had planned on using.

The outdoor art show! Why, that was like a carnival — no one in town missed it, even the kids. I should say especially the kids. The sidewalks are all strung with paintings and drawings, and sometimes they get so crowded you have to walk in the street. That's when we see all the kids from town and find out all the summer gossip. They sell cotton candy and ice cream and have band concerts, and they give prizes for all the artwork: paintings, handmade jewelry, sculpture, all that. There are always articles and pictures in the paper about it, and none of the kids would miss it for the world. Lots of artists from the towns nearby show their work, too, but my friends and I never paid much attention to who they were. We were too interested in just having fun and looking at some of the nice pictures. I was worried for a minute that Mrs. Folsom might run into someone who knew me, but then I realized that no one could possibly recognize me from that painting.

That night I told Grandma and Grandpa and Peter that my portrait was going to be in the outdoor art show.

"Aw, big deal!" Peter said.

"Now, Peter," Grandpa said sternly, "you should be happy for your sister. 'The truest mark of being born with good qualities is being born without envy.'"

"Envy!" he shrieked. "Who would want to have your picture by one of those lady artists in the outdoor art show for everyone to see! Gross!"

But Grandma just smiled. "Well, I for one would be very proud. And as for you, young man, if someone did a picture of you holding one of your big catches, I don't think you'd mind a bit! Now have some more of this nice chicken and broccoli. It's just full of wonderful vitamins and minerals."

That was about the only thing that the four of us did together: eat. And watch TV. Of course sometimes Peter and I would play games together, too, but we usually didn't finish them because somewhere in the middle we'd get into a fight about cheating or the score, and before one of us just about killed the other, Grandpa would come to break it up with threats of dumb kinds of punishments and a whole big mess of choice sayings. What really stopped us wasn't the fear of not being able to watch TV, but not wanting to hear anymore proverbs.

I was so used to those proverbs, though, that a few of them slipped out when I was with Mrs. Folsom, and she would always look surprised.

"Where in the world did you hear that?" she asked the first time I told Tommy, "Waste not, want not," after he left his cupcake on the grass.

"From my grandmother," I replied.

"Oh, that figures. I didn't think from your mother."

I froze, realizing I'd better be careful. I had never mentioned Grandma before. But everyone had grandmothers, and they were supposed to be old-fashioned.

Those old sayings must have become part of me, though, because the next week I was right there with "Haste makes waste." I felt my face getting hot, but Mrs. Folsom just said, "Ugh! Your grandmother again! Do you see her often, Kitten?"

Did you ever hear your voice saying something that you weren't able to stop — almost like it was somebody else talking? Mine was saying now, "Sometimes in the summer I stay with them, and we often visit on weekends. They have a farm, with a brook and ponies, and it's so much fun!" I wanted to bite my tongue out, but it was too late. I just couldn't help myself. If I hadn't said those things, I would have started to make all kinds of explanations about who my family really was, and it was way too late now. It was easier just to go on like this.

"My!" she said. "You certainly lead a colorful, active life, don't you!" She had a funny look on her face when she said it, almost as if she was, well, jealous. Then I remembered what she had told me while she was painting me about how poor she was when she was a little girl. I wished with all my heart that I could have said to her, "Well, don't feel bad. You only had one doll, but you had a mother and father. There's all kinds of ways of being poor." Then I had to laugh, because that sounded like one of Grandma's sayings. Who knows, maybe it was. They really did get into my blood!

4

Mrs. Folsom looked funny when she opened the door for me the next morning, as though something special had happened. But before she could say a word, Tommy grabbed me around the knees and cried, "We're going away for a week. To a lake with boats!"

All I could manage was "Huh?" and then I lost my balance and was just about to fall *kerplunk*, right on top of him. But Mrs. Folsom grabbed me on my way down and instead I kind of fell into her arms, and Tommy crouched down on the floor laughing with delight. Mrs. Folsom smelled so pretty, and it was such a nice feeling having her arms around me like that. Then she grabbed Tommy and swung him up high. "Hey, you, you're a little young for tackle football!" she told him. Suddenly she turned around to me, still holding Tommy, and said, "Oh, Kitten, I'm so excited, I just couldn't wait to tell you! My husband decided to take an extra week of vacation, and we've just planned a trip to Maine. The Clintons — you know, Paula Clinton often comes here with her daughter Marcy — well, we're renting cottages on a lake, right next to each other, and there are boats and waterskiing and swimming and outdoor barbecues. . . ." Her voice trailed off and she kept looking at me in this funny way, but I was busy biting my cheeks inside to try not to burst out crying. It sounded like a dream — the kind of dream other people's families lived. And on top of that I would be stuck at home with absolutely nothing to do. I wouldn't even be earning money!

I started blinking and forced a smile to try to hide how crushed I was. "Boy, that sounds wonderful, Mrs. Folsom! You'll have the greatest time." My voice came out sounding awfully queer, though.

She was still looking at me strangely. "Kitten, do you think your family might let you come along? It'll be next week."

My mouth just sort of dropped open, but I couldn't talk. Mrs. Folsom went on, "Oh, Kitten, please try to talk them into it. We'll take the *best* care of you! You see, the Clintons are bringing along a mother's helper for Marcy, and we thought if you could come and take care of Tommy for us, it would be just perfect. The other girl is just your age — Lulu Phelps. Do you know her?"

I managed to shake my head no, and she hurried on, "Her family just moved to town about a month ago and she started working for Paula and Wally last week. They already made the arrangements with her and her parents last night, but I wanted to wait till today when you came to talk to you about it. I know how close your family is and how you always do things together, but it would just be for one week. We've never done anything like this before. We usually take traveling vacations and leave Tommy home with a nurse, but this sounds like so much fun. And I know you'll enjoy it, Kitten! You'll be part of the family, of course, just as Lulu will, and you'll both have plenty of time for yourselves. In fact you'll do less baby-sitting during the day, but naturally we'll be going out at night and you and Lulu will stay with the kids. But the owners of the place have their own cottage right there, too, and they agreed to be available every evening if you and Lulu should need them for any reason. There will always be adults around — I want to make sure your parents understand that. And your pay would be fifty dollars for the week. Well" — and she looked at me expectantly — "what do you think, Kitten?"

I didn't answer right away because I didn't trust my voice. I just looked back and forth between Mrs. Folsom and Tommy.

"I'd love to," I said finally. "It sounds like fun. And I'm sure my — parents will let me." Now I grinned. "At least I sure hope so!"

"To *Maine*?" Grandma gasped. "Well, I don't know. That's awfully far, isn't it?"

"We're not going to walk," I pointed out. "We're driving. In their Cadillac."

Grandma lowered her eyelids, the way she does when she's taken by surprise and trying to decide on something. "Well," she said at last, "I don't know — I'll have to talk it over with Grandpa, of course." She thought for a moment longer, probably about all the wonderful plans I had told her about, then she said, "It is a big responsibility for them, but" —

and now she smiled at me — "it's a grand opportunity for you to see something of the world. After all, man is as broad as his own horizons. Your grandfather and I do our best to broaden your lives, yours and Peter's, but it's hard, don't you know. When people get older . . ." She turned away and all of a sudden I felt very sorry for her. She and Grandpa loved us so much, and I think they knew that we sometimes minded not having young parents like other kids did.

But afterward it was like Christmas in July. Grandma and Grandpa asked me a thousand questions about the plans, some over and over again, but I didn't mind, and then they finally said okay. *I could go.* Grandma said to have Mrs. Folsom call her tomorrow to talk over plans. I knew I'd have to figure out a way around that pretty quick.

I had just brushed my teeth and put on my nightgown, when the phone rang. I was sure it must be Mrs. Folsom, and when Peter beat me to the phone I wanted to kill him. What if she got into a conversation with him and he told her the truth about our family? But it was Charlie calling him, and all we could hear was, "Hey, great! Hey, great great great!"

When he hung up the phone, he started

screaming, "Yee-ee-ee!" and running around the dining-room table like a nut. Honestly I don't remember ever seeing him so excited, but I could have killed him for making me wait so long to find out why. Finally when he hardly had any breath left, he said, "Charlie's father is taking him on a fishing trip to Cape Cod — for a whole weekend. And guess what? He said Charlie could invite a friend along. And guess who he invited?"

"Skint?" I asked innocently.

"No, you dope, why would I be so — oh, *you know*!"

Grandpa caught hold of his arm and looked down at him happily. "Say, now that is grand news, Peter. That's real nice of Charlie's folks."

"And Charlie," I put in.

"It certainly is," Grandma said, putting an arm around Peter. "Will it be this weekend, dear?"

Peter's face suddenly went blank. "Gee, I don't remember. I think so — or did he say next weekend? Or the *next*?"

When I burst out laughing, he glared at me. "All you do is make fun of me. You think you're such a big shot because you have a job and you got asked to go to Maine and everything. Well, ha-ha on you, I got invited on a vacation, too, and by my *best* friend, and I'm going to have more fun than you."

From the looks on Grandma and Grandpa's faces you'd think we were fighting with them instead of each other. "For goodness sake, Peter," I said, wanting to end it, "what's the matter with you? I'm glad you're going! I think it's great. I'm real happy for you."

"Of course she is, Peter," Grandma said now, hugging him to her. "We all are. It's just like I was telling Kitten this afternoon when she told me about the Folsoms inviting her on their trip — we're happy to see you children happy. Grandpa and I are just sorry we can't do things like that with you, but you see, somehow the Lord provides."

Peter blinked a few times and honestly, I felt like going over and hugging him, too. But I knew he would be embarrassed. He looked straight at me and said, "Well, thanks. I'm glad for you, too, Kitten. I guess we're both pretty lucky, aren't we?"

"Yes." I looked past him and Grandma and Grandpa, sort of into the wall and past it. "I guess we are."

"I mean, even if we don't have our own families — " He stopped, then added, "I mean

51

parents, we have our grandparents and good friends. Why, that's more family even than lots of kids have."

Peter and I got out of the room fast, because we hated it when Grandma tried to keep herself from crying and Grandpa got that funny look in his eyes. "Hey!" Peter yelled, heading for the phone. "I have to call Charlie back and find out which weekend it is!"

It was the weekend after next. That meant that Peter and I would both be coming home from our vacations at the same time. That kind of excited us, and I stayed up late in his room that night so we could talk about it. It was fun and we were laughing and thinking of silly things like what if our cars passed each other on the highway. Then all of a sudden, just as I was thinking that gee, Peter was a pretty good kid, and I guessed I was lucky to even have a brother at all, he said, "Hey, you're nice. I don't think I'd want anyone else for a sister." I almost couldn't believe my ears. It was as if he'd read my mind or I'd read his or something. Anyway it was nice and I said, "Thanks, same to you." I laid my head on the foot of his bed — he'd been sitting up in his bed and I'd been sitting cross-legged on the floor — and all of a sudden I felt so tired I just couldn't hold my head up any longer. The next day Grandma told me that Peter had fallen asleep with his head right next to mine. I was positive she'd say, "Blood is thicker than water," one of her big favorites, but maybe she just saved that for our fights. Actually she didn't quote anything. She just smiled down at me in that corny way that grown-ups have, and I was glad I had to leave right away to get to work.

"Well, what did they say?" Mrs. Folsom asked practically before I was through the door.

I had thought up a perfect story on the way over. "They said yes. My mother tried to phone you, but your line was busy, and then she and Daddy had to go out. She made me promise to tell you that it will be fine and — and she's sure everything will work out okay. She said she would try calling you again."

"Oh, that's wonderful, Kitten!" She squeezed my hand so hard it hurt, and it was funny to think that she was almost as happy about it as I was. "Look, maybe I ought to phone her now," she added. "What's your number, Kitten?"

"Oh, she's not home — she went to the store when I left."

She snapped her fingers. "I know — I'll write her a note. I really should have thought of that." She went over to her desk and wrote quickly on one of her little flowered note pads that said FROM THE DESK OF VERA FOLSOM. She tore it off, folded it, and handed it to me, and I put it in my pocket. But as soon as she went out I looked at it and breathed a sigh of relief. It said:

> *Thank you so much for letting Kitten come to Maine with us next week. We'll take good care of her and I know she'll have a wonderful time.*
>
> *V.F.*

Everything was working out perfectly. Now she and Grandma wouldn't ever have to talk on the phone. Grandma would probably just send a little note back with me, the way she did to school for trips.

And then something even more wonderful happened that very afternoon. I met Lulu.

She came over with Marcy after naptime, and when Mrs. Folsom introduced us I looked at this girl and thought, she's awfully cute. I bet she's a snob. Then when she said, "Hey, I'm pleased to meet you," with such a thick southern accent you could have cut it with a knife, I knew I must be right. She had beautiful golden-brown hair that curled around her shoulders, and eyes that looked like brown velvet buttons. And when she smiled, which she seemed to do most of the time, she had these big dimples.

I said something like "Me too," and soon we were in a big conversation about where we lived, and then I found out that she still didn't know her way around Sun Haven very well because she'd moved up here from South Carolina. She started asking me all kinds of questions, about myself and the Folsoms and Tommy and school — what was it like and where was it and everything. At least when Marcy and Tommy let us get a word in edgewise. They kept at us all the time. Between Marcy being crazy about Lulu and Tommy about me, it was like some kind of contest to see whose baby-sitter was better, and we all ended up laughing and tumbling around on the floor. When it was time for Lulu to take Marcy home, Mrs. Folsom came back in and said, "Kitten, would you mind taking Tommy over to the Clintons'? He'll play with Marcy till dinnertime, and then I'll run over and pick him up. You can just go straight home from there."

"I'm lucky I met you today, Kitten," Lulu said after we left. "I don't know any kids in Sun Haven and I was feeling so lost! I'm going to need you a whole lot, especially when school starts. You'll have to be my little old guide dog!"

I laughed, because that was the last thing in the world Lulu needed. I just had the feeling about her that new or not she'd find her way around awfully fast. But at the same time it made me feel so good when she said she needed me. Nobody ever said anything like that before. And to hear it from someone like Lulu made me feel important in a way that was new to me. I wanted so much to be good friends with her.

"I'm glad Mrs. Folsom asked you to walk us along," Lulu said, smiling with her dimples. "After all, we'll be seeing lots of each other next week in Maine, and I wanted so bad to get to know you before." She said "bad" like it was two words — bay-ed — the way she did with a lot of words, and I had to smile at it. You just couldn't help liking this girl. It was as if I'd just gone crazy for Lulu the first moment I saw her — which I really didn't. But I knew then I sure had been wrong about her. She was anything but a snob!

"We can have a ball together up there!" she said, grabbing my hand and giving it a squeeze. "Are you a good swimmer? I have a lifesaver badge. Do you like fishing? My brothers are fishing nuts, but I just like it so-so. Steve — that's my big brother, he's thirteen — learned to sail last summer and he promised to teach me. I wish I could learn before we go, but I guess there won't be time. Hey, Kitten — gee, that's such a cute name! Can you imagine having a name like *Lulu*? The only thing worse is my *real* name, Louise. *Yu-uch!* Imagine saying my name is *Louise* Phelps! It sounds like a teacher or something, doesn't it?"

"I don't know," I said. "It sounds like a nice name to me. But I do think Lulu fits you better."

"Well, Kitten fits you, too. Cute, like you. Hey, what's *your* real name?"

She really went for that story about my name. Soon we found out about each other's families. She had another brother, Alfie, who was nine, and a fifteen-year-old sister, Arletta.

I just told her I lived with my grandparents and Peter. If she was going to be my friend, she'd have to know the truth about me. I didn't think Mrs. Folsom would ever get to talking to Lulu about my family, but just in case I planned to warn her once I knew her better.

The strange thing was that the more we talked, the more we seemed to have in common. When I told her about Peter and how all he ever did was go fishing, she said so did Alfie. "Do you believe we both have brothers the same age who are fishing nuts?" I asked.

"Oh, Alfie's okay, but he can be a pest sometimes."

"Peter, too! In fact that's what I call him — Peter the Pest! Hey, I wonder if they'd like each other."

"We'll have to get them to meet. Alfie's met a few kids around our house, but none of them go fishing."

"Oh, Peter goes every day. Do you know what happened to him?" I told her about Charlie's invitation and Lulu smiled.

"I guess Peter's lucky to have such a good friend," she said.

I giggled. "You're beginning to sound like my grandmother."

"Your *grandmother*!"

I told Lulu then about Grandma and

Grandpa's way of talking in sayings all the time, and she said, "Oh, they sound neat. I can't wait to meet them!"

By then we had left the Clintons' and were walking home. We only lived about five blocks away from each other, but after a few blocks we had to separate and go in different directions.

"Look, Kitten," she said as we reached the parting point, "supposing you come by the Clintons' tomorrow after work and pick me up and come on home with me. My family'd love to meet you, and we've got lots of planning to do together for next week — what clothes to take along and everything. Tell your grandmamma you're going to be staying on to have dinner with us, and I'll walk you home before dark, or if my daddy's around he'll drive you. Hear?"

"Well — well, I don't know. I mean, I'm not sure." To dinner! Ann and Jeannie and lots of other kids I knew did that kind of thing, but I couldn't remember the last time I ate at someone else's house. I felt flattered to be invited.

I tried to shrug in a casual way. "I'll have to ask my grandmother. Tell me your phone number, and I'll call you later."

I said it over and over to myself all the way home, and without even saying hello to Grandma I ran over to the phone and wrote it down on the message pad. Then I said, "Hi, Grandma. Guess what? I'm invited for dinner tomorrow night."

She beamed. "At the Folsoms'?"

"No, at Lulu's. My new friend."

She shook her head, but she was smiling. "Well, now let's hear all about *this* one. 'Child, thou are wealthy in thy friends.'"

I thought about that saying while I was lying in bed remembering all the wonderful things about that day, and I realized it was true. After a last, happy review of all my good luck — mainly the Folsoms and Lulu — I turned over, cuddled into my pillow, and opened the door to my Family. I'd been so busy lately that I'd hardly talked to them at all.

5

As I followed Lulu up the creaky porch steps
to her house, I heard this really loud music
blasting through the front screen door. Lulu
took my hand and led me inside, and at first
I couldn't see very well because my eyes were
still blinded by the bright sunshine from
outdoors, and it was so much darker inside.
But after I blinked a few times, I realized that
all those clumps I saw around the room were
a mixture of people and furniture. They
looked like teen-agers, maybe they were a
few years older than me. Now, I'm not shy
or anything — I mean not *really*. But I wanted

to go right through the floor! Everyone turned around and stared at me.

"Arletta, this is Kitten, my new friend I told you about." She pulled me forward. "Kitten, this is my big sister, Arletta."

Some of the boys and girls called out, "Hi, Lulu," "How's the breadwinner?" and things like that. A couple looked at me with a quick, passing interest, but Arletta seemed really glad I was there. "Lulu's told me about you, Kitten. It's really nice to meet you."

"Thank you," I said. I wanted to say something nice but I didn't know how.

Lulu was getting impatient. "Come on, I'll take you to meet Mama and the boys. They're probably in the kitchen."

"Arletta sure has a lot of friends," I said.

Lulu nodded. "She met them at Sam's Snack Shop the second day we were here. It never takes Arletta long to meet people."

The kitchen was so tiny and dark that I wondered how anyone could cook there. But pots were steaming on the stove, and Lulu's mother seemed perfectly comfortable. She was a big, sort of fat woman with lots of dark hair.

"Mama, this is Kitten!" Lulu said proudly. Her mother plunked down the mixing bowl she'd been holding and rushed toward me so that I really got scared.

"Well, Kitten, how wonderful to meet you! Why, Lulu's been chattering away about you ever since yesterday — being new in town and all, and here by this big coincidence she meets another little girl like herself, and to think you're both going to have yourselves a vacation way up in Vermont with those lovely — "

"Maine, Mama," Lulu said, laughing.

"Oh, yes, Maine. Well, it's all the same to me!" She stepped back to smile at me, and now as I looked at her I saw she had a pretty face underneath all that hair, and nice warm brown eyes. "Now, look, why don't you sit yourselves down here and have some soda pop and snacks."

On the table there was a bowl full of popcorn and cheese sticks and three big bottles of soda. Lulu got glasses for us, and as she was pouring, the kitchen door flew open and a fat boy with blond hair and a red face rushed in waving a great big flopping fish around and screaming, "Lookee, lookee, lookee what I got!" Mrs. Phelps let out a screech, and then she and Lulu were out of their chairs and around him in a flash. *So that*, I thought as I watched with a warm, nice kind of feeling, *is*

Alfie. I wonder if he's as much of a pest as Peter. Just then Lulu's older brother, Steve, came in and was introduced, and all the other kids came piling in from the living room, and it was like a mob scene, with everyone yelling, "Let's see!" and "Hey, how about that!" and "Alfie's finally made a killing!"

As soon as the excitement died down, Mrs. Phelps turned to me suddenly and cried, "Kitten, darling, you must stay for dinner! We have this great big fish, and we'll have a real celebration. I was right in the middle of making chicken dumplings, but we can have that, too. Now, why don't you go over to the telephone and call your mama and — "

"Mama!" Lulu cut in. "I already invited her to dinner — remember, I told you last night? And she called and said she could?"

Mrs. Phelps giggled, "Oh, heavens, where *is* my head! Why, of course, we certainly were expecting you! Now you must make yourself at home here."

She went over to the stove, glancing at Alfie who was busy cleaning his fish at the sink while he babbled away to Steve with all the details of how he'd caught it.

"Come on," Lulu said, taking my hand, "let's go up to my room. Mama," she called back over her shoulder, "please call us when it's time to set the table."

I couldn't really believe Lulu's room. The same feeling I had when I came into her house of everything being such a jumble hit me again, and I didn't know where to start looking. I guess it was because Grandma was so neat and orderly, and Mrs. Folsom's house was always super-perfect. Even Tommy's room when all the toys were spread around didn't look like this. Lulu's room only had a bed that was half-made and a dresser with some knobs missing. Hanging above it was a big mirror with strange streaks in it that made you look funny, and in the corner was a kitchen chair piled with clothes. Cartons and plastic bags filled with all different kinds of things were piled against one wall, and the closet door was partly open because a hinge was broken.

Lulu swept her hand about, explaining, "We haven't had a chance to fix up the house or even unpack everything yet. There are still cartons all over, and we're supposed to get some new furniture and things, so it's a little messy yet." She looked at me kind of funny and I said, "Well, you've only been here a month, what do you expect? It takes time to get settled. Besides I *like* your room. You're lucky to have it all to yourself."

"I know." She seemed grateful that I understood. "Arletta has her own room, too, and the boys have one together."

My eye caught some sparkling things glittering on top of her dresser, and I just couldn't help going over to see what they were. It was a whole big mess of necklaces, rings, pins, and earrings made out of all different pretty things — colored stones, pearls, silver, gold. "Are these yours?" I asked. I'd never seen so much jewelry all together outside of a store.

Lulu laughed. "Yes, but none of it is real, you know."

"Well, I didn't think they were real *jewels*. But my goodness, I never saw so much — I mean no kid I ever knew had so much. Are they yours?"

"Of course! Lots of these are things Arletta gave me when she was tired of them and Mama, too, and the rest is the stuff Daddy brings home on paydays." She grinned. "Woolworth's best."

"Oh. Well, that's real nice that your father brings you presents."

Lulu shrugged. "It's like a tradition, I guess.

But I don't think he'll do it so much now. Things are sort of tight."

"What does your father do?" I asked.

"He's going to be a field representative or something important like that for this big insurance company. That's why we moved up here. Right now he's in their training program, but as soon as he finishes we'll be on Easy Street!"

I'd never heard of it. "Is that in Sun Haven?"

Lulu shrieked with laughter. "Kitten, are you serious? That's just an expression! It means we'll, you know, have made it big."

I slapped my hand to my head. "Oh no, not you, too, with expressions!"

"What do you mean?"

I told her again about Grandma and Grandpa and their sayings for every occasion. "If I'm looking for a missing sock, it's 'Seek and ye shall find,' or if I asked about something they don't want me to know, they just answer, 'Curiosity killed the cat.' When I was little my grandmother was talking about The Tragedy that happened to my mother and father, and she told someone, 'Gladly my cross I'd bear,' and it wasn't till about last year that I knew what she meant. I thought she said, 'Gladly my cross-eyed bear,' and I thought it was so cute I always went around saying it."

Lulu smiled and slipped her arm through mine. Her face had turned all soft and serious now. "Kitten," she said, "I'm going to be that curious cat and ask you some questions about *your* family. Whatever did happen to your — poor mama and papa?"

Usually I don't like to talk about my parents, and my friends just sort of naturally steer away from the subject. But Lulu had been so open with me that I wanted to tell her. "They were killed in a car crash. I was four and my brother was two. I remember them, but he doesn't. He thinks he does, but it's probably from all the stories I used to tell him about them and all the pictures we have around of them. Mom looked like me, only much prettier. I remember her smile and how she used to read to me at night. My father was big and laughed a lot. Once he took me to the circus. But that's about all I really can remember about that time — in a way it seems like we've always lived with Grandma and Grandpa. They never like to talk about the accident, though. They just call it The Tragedy if they have to mention it, so I guess we've kind of gotten into that habit, too." Lulu's face looked worried so I squeezed her arm to reassure her. "Oh, I'm used to it. Grandma and Grandpa are really very good to us, even though they are old and awfully old-fashioned. Besides I sort of make up for it. I have this wonderful secret family of my very own. If I tell you about it, will you promise not to laugh at me?"

Lulu's eyes widened. "Why, Kitten, of course I wouldn't laugh at you. I think you're really interesting, that's what I think!"

Interesting! No one had ever called me that before! I smiled the warmth of my happiness to her. "Thank you. I just had the feeling I could tell you all this. You see, I've never ever told anybody in the whole world. So you must promise one more thing: to keep it a solemn secret and not tell a soul, not any of your family or your very closest friend."

"I promise, Kitten. I'll keep your secret till I die! And you and I are going to be best friends — don't you know that by now?"

I felt funny and looked around the room quickly, just to sort of get my balance, and the crazy thought came to me: *I never knew Heaven was such a cluttered place.* I took a deep breath, then looked straight at Lulu, but when I opened my mouth to tell her about my

Family, all that came out was, "Are you *sure* you won't think I'm cuckoo?" But she nodded so seriously that soon all the words came tumbling out, and before I could take another breath, I had told her all about Mums and Daddy and Buck and Gaby. And then I was able to tell her how I'd told Mrs. Folsom about them instead of my real family.

When I finished she let out a big sigh. "Well, I think that's a beautiful story! Why shouldn't you have a family like that to make up for what was taken away from you? Oh, Kitten, of course I'll keep your secret! You can count on me forever."

I felt good about telling her. Besides everything else now, I wouldn't have to worry about anything slipping out next week when we'd all be together in Maine. And when the summer was over and my job was up with the Folsoms, nothing would make any difference about my daydreams anyway. Till then Mrs. Folsom just knew me in a different way — that was all.

Lulu was looking at me funny. "Kitten, since you told me such a deep secret and we're going to be best friends, I'm going to tell you the secret about my family. Daddy's job really isn't that important. Oh, it might be, if we're lucky. But he's had about a million jobs ever since I can remember. Nothing seems to work out. And he's so smart. He went to college and everything. But you'll see, moving up here is going to change his luck! We all feel it in our bones. Listen" — and her mood suddenly changed — "how would you like to fool around with this stuff?" She ran over to her dresser, pointing at rows of little bottles and jars and tubes.

"What is it?" I asked.

"Arletta's old makeup. Would you like to put some on?" My surprise must have crept all over my face because she burst out laughing when she looked at me. "Oh, don't worry, I'm not allowed to wear it! I just fool around with it. I have lots of nail polish, too."

"Oooh, I'd *love* to! But is there time? What if your mother calls us down right in the middle?"

Lulu frowned. "You're right, I think it's too late. Look, why don't we save it till next time? I think she's going to call us soon. Let's make a list of what to take to Maine next week instead." She rummaged around in a drawer and triumphantly pulled out a writing pad and pencil. "And I'll tell you what, Kitten, I'll bring this stuff along, and we can do it up there when our folks are gone."

"Yes, let's!"

"Okay, now let's start on our list."

We covered two pages by the time Mrs. Phelps's voice drifted up to us: "Girls, it's time to set up for dinner!" When we got down to the kitchen Arletta was mixing something in a huge bowl and Mrs. Phelps was frying fish in a gigantic cloud of steam. Lulu led me to the dining room, where Steve and Alfie were placing chairs around a big table with funny carved legs and a scarred top. The chairs looked funny together — half of them were real fancy with worn, velvet seats and carved legs like on the table, and the other half were modern with plastic seat covers. The pretty lace tablecloth that Mrs. Phelps handed me looked so real I was surprised to feel that it was plastic. Lulu and I spread it on the table, and Mrs. Phelps came back in with a little vase of straw flowers that she put in the middle, while Lulu took two candles in bright blue holders from the sideboard and placed them on each side of the vase. Suddenly the table looked so pretty! Then she took out a stack of dinner plates, and as I helped her spread them around, I discovered that there were three different styles. Hardly any of the silverware matched either. "Oh!" Lulu cried. "I forgot the napkins!" She opened another drawer and took out a pile of neatly folded, snowy-white linen napkins. When she turned back to the drawer, I felt them to make sure they were really cloth, and then she took out some big silver rings.

"What are those?" I asked.

Her eyes widened. "Why, they're napkin rings." She turned one around fondly in her fingers. "Mama and Daddy got these for their wedding from Grandma Phelps. They're *sterling silver!*" She pointed to the engraved design that I hadn't noticed, as it was pretty worn. "That's their initials — AHP — Angela and Hanson Phelps. Oh, I'll have to show you some of the other things Grandma Phelps gave us. They're all *real expensive.*" As she showed me how to put the napkins into the shining rings, a car horn suddenly blared outside.

"Daddy's home — come on!" Lulu cried, grabbing my hand and pulling me toward the living room. By the time we got to the entrance hall it was crowded with the whole family. Steve, Alfie, Arletta, and Mrs. Phelps all rushed toward the man who was standing next to the car, scooping out packages and paper bags of all sizes and colors. Steve got there first, but the rest weren't far behind, and everyone started grabbing packages and running back up into the house with them. But Mrs. Phelps was just standing there, her hands on her hips, her hair flying, and her dimples etched into her cheeks like gashes as she grinned at her husband.

"Come on," Lulu called to me, holding open the screen door, and I followed her into the living room where all the packages had been dumped, right in the middle of the floor.

"Anyone got a match?" Steve asked, and we all laughed. Mr. and Mrs. Phelps walked into the room then, arms around each other and smiling happily. He was about as tall as his wife, but very skinny, with not very much hair and funny, round, wire-rimmed glasses. His suit was a little rumpled, but somehow he looked very neat and dressed up on this summer day, with a tie and long-sleeved shirt that had shiny cuff links.

All the children crowded around them and everyone was talking at once, begging to see what was in the packages and asking did he get him or her this or that special thing. And then he started handing out the bags, like a

Santa Claus in a firehouse I once visited at Christmastime. Paper started flying and there were squeals of "Ooh — look at this! Just what I wanted!" and things like that. Lulu already had a collection of barrettes, ball-point pens, knee socks, and bubble bath. Everyone was jabbering away and all of a sudden all eyes were on me, and Mr. Phelps was saying, " — and no one even introduced me to Lulu's friend!"

I giggled as Lulu grabbed my hand and pulled me over close to him. "Oh, Daddy, in all the excitement I forgot. Kitten," and she turned to me, her eyes sparkling, "this is my daddy. He always goes on a big spree when he gets a new job. Daddy" — and she turned to him, still clutching my hand — "this is Kitten Tate. Her real name is Carol Ann, but everyone calls her Kitten. And she's my best friend."

Mr. Phelps took my other hand and lifting it up, kissed it the way people do to royalty, bowing his head so I could see the pink spaces between his blondish hairs. "I'm ever so honored to meet you, Miss Carol Ann Kitten Tate," he said. "Welcome to our humble home." Then he turned around and, looking over the mound of still-unopened packages, picked up a tiny little green bag and handed it to me. "And this is for you."

"Oh, Mr. Phelps, it's really all right, you don't have to — "

But his raised hand stopped me. "Never mind, it's only a little token for you to share in our pleasure."

"Oh, thank you very much. And it's so nice to meet you, too!" I opened the bag and pulled out a beautiful silvery pendant on a big chain. Arletta and Lulu loved it, but not more than I did, and as they slipped it over my head, I felt sort of bad because I knew that it had been meant for one of them and I wondered if they were mad about it. But they really didn't seem to be.

As we sat around the dining table stuffing ourselves with the most delicious fried fish I ever tasted and absolutely wonderful chicken dumplings and salad and hot biscuits, I was happier than I'd been in a long time. Lulu and her family fussed over me as if I was somebody important and kept filling up my plate until I just had to stop eating, and they asked me lots of questions about Sun Haven and what the kids did for fun, but not things about my family the way some grown-ups do. Why, they made me feel practically like a celebrity in one way. And in another I almost felt as if I belonged to their family, even though I'd only known them a few hours. It's funny, but I never felt that way in any of my other friends' houses or anywhere else. Even the Folsoms'. I felt like part of their family there, too, but in a different way — in the way that I belonged to them only because I was taking care of Tommy. When I left their house each day, I wasn't sure they ever gave me a second thought. But I had the feeling it would be different with the Phelpses. That I would be someone special even when I wasn't around, because I was special to Lulu. I figured it was a certain something that some families have, and it was the first time in my life I'd ever bumped up against it.

Mr. Phelps drove me home when it started getting dark, and of course Lulu came along in the car. When I asked if she could come in, Mr. Phelps said it was too late, that they had to stop off at the drugstore before it closed. So we planned for her to come to my house the next day after work. But the funniest thing happened that night. It was when I was in bed, all snuggled down into my pillow the way I like to, and I let my whole mind relax and sort of drift into the life of my Family —

I just find myself there with them, and the ideas just come up by themselves. But this night it didn't work. I let myself drift and relax, but all I could think about was Lulu and her family, and my stubborn mind went over every single thing that had happened from the moment we ran up those creaky steps to her house. The last thing I remembered thinking about was the ride home in the car, with Mr. Phelps and Lulu joking about Alfie's fish and saying he'd probably gone and bought it at the A & P.

6

When Lulu came home with me the next
afternoon, I could see right away that
Grandma liked her. Well, she didn't *not* like
her, if you know what I mean. She gave us
milk and cookies she'd baked that morning
and asked Lulu lots of questions about herself
and her family. Lulu was polite, but sometimes
she would make some funny cracks, like when
Grandma asked what a field representative
did, Lulu said, "I'm not really sure, but it
sounds to me like maybe he represents a field."
Grandma didn't think that was very funny,
but Peter did. He actually choked on a cookie,
and Lulu and I started pounding him on the

back till Grandma yanked us away and pulled his arms straight up in the air, mumbling, "Vain is the help of man." Lulu winked at me and I had to put my hand over my mouth to keep from laughing. But Peter got over it very fast and he kept asking questions, too, especially when he found out about Alfie and his fishing. In fact there was a while there when he and Lulu were talking together so much, I was starting to feel like the outsider.

"Hey, why don't you go over to meet Alfie?" I piped up and Lulu said, "Yes, you must, Peter! I know you'd like each other!"

We asked Grandma if it was okay to go and promised to be back in time for dinner. On the way over, I never heard Peter babble so much. He told Lulu about the trip to Cape Cod and about all his favorite fishing spots. I could hardly get a word in edgewise, and all I could think of was, wouldn't it be funny if he and Alfie hated each other?

But they didn't. They talked about just what you'd expect them to, while Lulu and I left them and ran up to her room. She pulled out an open suitcase from under her bed to show me what she had already packed for our trip, and then I copied the list we had made together, adding the things we had thought of since. By then it was time to go, and when we went downstairs to get Peter, Mrs. Phelps came in and gave me such a big greeting you'd think I was their long-lost cousin. She told me what a cute little brother I had, and wasn't it nice that he came to meet Alfie.

"I'm going to take him to Bulldog Creek tomorrow," Peter told me on the way home.

"Who — Alfie?"

"Of course. We're going real early — it's the best of all my places. I promised him a good catch."

I laughed. "What if you can't keep your promise?"

He shrugged. "Oh, well, we'll catch frogs or something. You can't win 'em all, you know! Hey, he's nice. I'm glad you met him for me, Kitten. Now I have a new friend, too."

He had such a happy smile on his face I wanted to hug him. But I wouldn't dare.

"Footloose and fancy-free," Grandma said when I asked her how she like Lulu. "That's how she strikes me, if you want the truth. But she's a friendly little girl. A person can't help liking her."

Peter made faces behind her back and I laughed. There was no question that Peter liked Lulu, all right. I wished that Grandma would treat Lulu the way her family treated me, but of course I knew that was impossible, even if she was crazy about her. Grandma just wasn't like that.

With each day I got more excited about our trip. Everything was working out so great. Grandma had done just what I expected: after I gave her Mrs. Folsom's note she wrote an answer for me to take over. Grandma always tried to do what she thought was the "correct thing." If people phoned her, she would phone them back, and if someone wrote to her, she would write back. So she wrote this nice, polite note that thanked Mrs. Folsom for inviting me to Maine. She said that I loved working there, and that they always enjoyed hearing the nice little stories I had to tell about Tommy. There was absolutely nothing in that letter that I wouldn't have wanted Mrs. Folsom to see. Except the signature. At first I was just going to say to Mrs. Folsom that my mother had told me to tell her — and then I would repeat all those things. But I was afraid it might sound fishy. And what if they ever *did* get to talk to each other and Grandma mentioned the note. . . .

"What am I going to do?" I wailed to Lulu the next day, showing it to her.

She read it carefully. "Why, it's perfectly fine, Kitten! She never says 'my granddaughter,' or anything like that. What's wrong with — oh! Oh, I see! The name! Nora Herbert. That's right, it's your *mama's* parents, isn't it. . . Hey!" Suddenly she clapped her hands together in triumph. "I've got it, Kitten! Just write *Tate* after her name. *Nora Herbert Tate*. Lots of women sign their names like that. Didn't you ever notice? Why, some women keep using their own names after they get married without using their husband's names. And I think that some men even take their wives' names."

That was the thing about Lulu, I thought then. She was so much more worldly than I was — or probably ever would be! It just never would have occurred to me even to think of something like that. I looked at Grandma's note, then back up at Lulu. There was plenty of room after Grandma's signature, all right. But still . . .

"Come on, Kitten, don't be chicken! It's the only thing to do. Here, let's get a pen and practice. Just four letters — that's a cinch!"

In a while Lulu was able to copy Grandma's signature perfectly. Then she practiced writing *Tate* in the same style, and when she added it on with the same kind of blue ballpoint pen Grandma used, I couldn't tell the difference.

"Now," I groaned, "all I have to worry about is if either of them decides to call up the other one."

"Oh, that's easy," Lulu tossed off, "just say they're there for a visit."

"Grandma and Grandpa?"

Lulu nodded and I gasped. "Hey, that's it! They come down from their farm every year for a visit."

"A vacation!" Lulu added, her smile bright with excitement from the little twists we kept giving the story.

"Yes — a vacation. They stay with us kids while my parents go on their vacation. They'll be in charge!"

"Kitten, you are brilliant! Then if Mrs. Folsom does ever phone, she'll get your Grandma or Grandpa, who're taking over the household while Mr. and Mrs. Tate are flitting about Europe."

I giggled. "Oh, yes, flitting about Europe. That's what people like the Folsoms and Clintons always do, isn't it!"

"Anyway," Lulu was saying, "just take my word for it, Kitten. Everything's going to be fine. Aren't we geniuses the way we worked out this whole thing?"

I felt a little more like a storyteller than a genius. A storyteller — that's the word Grandma and Grandpa used for people who told what they called "harmless lies." I'd rather have thought of it as being a genius, the way Lulu said, but it bothered me because the truth of it was that it was real storytelling. I couldn't help myself, though. It was one of those things that had started out as real innocent and grew before I could stop it. But having Lulu be part of it now made it so much better. It was almost like a game. And whenever I felt awful about it, I'd remind myself it was a game that wasn't going to hurt anyone and would end when the summer was over.

I gave Mrs. Folsom the note and said a secret prayer. But she just smiled after she read it and said, "That's very nice. I guess we're all set now, aren't we?"

I waited till the next day to tell her the story about my grandparents coming. She was on her way into her studio to start her painting, and she just nodded and said, "Isn't that nice for everybody! Of course they know all about our arrangements for next week? Fine, then there won't be any problem."

Well, that settled that. I was able to pack with a free mind, and Lulu and I kept reminding each other about things to take that usually were already packed.

I went to Lulu's house every day after supper, and I was allowed to stay till just before it got dark. A few times Peter came along to visit with Alfie, too, and we always had fun walking home together and talking about Lulu's family. I loved being there and so did Peter. It was like going to a party — there were always so many people around and there was music and laughing and talking. Usually Lulu and I would go to her room because we always had so much to talk about in private. First we'd tell each other every single thing that happened that day at our jobs, and then we'd talk about our families and our friends and just about anything else that came into our minds. I told her I'd introduce her to Jeannie and Ann after we got back from Maine, and then I realized I'd been so busy with Lulu and plans for the trip that I hadn't even seen them the whole week! Suddenly my world just seemed too busy and exciting to be true. I never could remember a time like this, when the days weren't long enough! One of the nights Grandma told me

Jeannie and Ann had been over while I was at Lulu's, and then she gave me a saying about not dropping old friends for new ones. But how could I help it when I had someone like Lulu for a friend who just seemed to care about me more than they did? Besides, after that week I felt as though I knew Lulu better than Jeannie and Ann, with all the *real* talking we did. Anyway I told Grandma not to worry, that I wasn't dropping anyone, but that my life was just very busy right now.

Lulu and I tried to figure out a way to get the Clintons and the Folsoms to let us travel up together in the same car but it didn't work. "It's too bad one of them doesn't have a great big station wagon instead of those fancy Cadillacs!" Lulu said. "Then we could all pile in together the way our family does, and it would be a ball!"

But the funny thing was, the trip up with just me and the Folsoms was the best thing that could have happened, because I really got to be with them in a closer way. And after all, I was going to live with them for a week. Tommy wanted to be with me all the time. Of course we sat in the back together, but whenever we stopped for anything, to eat or rest, or get gas and use the rest rooms, it was always me he wanted to stay with and to take him. Dr. and Mrs. Folsom were glad because they knew that they'd be able to leave him with me a lot that week and go off on their own, and I was glad because — well, it was just a nice feeling being wanted like that.

But the trip itself was really fun. It took more than eight hours. It must have been one of the hottest days of the summer, and I sure blessed the car's air conditioning. It was awful whenever we stopped and had to get out and have the terrific heat hit us in the face. But once we got into Maine the roads were narrow and much slower than the superhighways we'd been riding on, and soon Dr. Folsom turned off the air conditioning and opened the windows. The air was fresh and sweet-smelling, and I loved looking at the pretty little towns we passed through. Some of them anyway. There were so many houses that looked like the kind you always see on Christmas cards. And the churches were small and simple and so pretty, too. But lots of the houses looked bare and poor. Those weren't much fun. Then we went through a town that smelled so awful we had to close the windows and hold our noses, and Tommy screamed and cried and nobody could quiet him until we finally passed that part and were able to let in the sweet, clean air again. Dr. Folsom said the bad smell was from the paper mill, and we all wondered what it must be like to live in those towns nearby and have that smell all the time, and Mrs. Folsom said, "Oh, well, I guess you get used to everything."

We all sort of groaned together and it made me feel so good. Dr. Folsom kept on saying funny things, and I wasn't scared of him any longer the way I used to be. At home he seemed so serious, even though he'd always smile at me and be friendly. But it was as if he was thinking of more important things, and I kind of felt like some little ant when he was around — which wasn't very often anyway. But on this trip he really turned out to be so different. They both seemed to be having such a good time just being together, and they kept including me in the conversation. Well, you can't imagine how *that* made me feel. I wanted to absolutely fly. And of course Tommy was at me all the time, so cute and cuddly. It was finally as if I really belonged with them. Why, it was almost the way I felt with my Family! I realized then that was probably why I hadn't even thought about Mums and Daddy and Buck and Gaby since the trip began. I remembered how Lulu and I had wanted so badly to travel up together, and it struck me now that if we had, I would have missed out on that special closeness I started feeling with the Folsoms. One of Grandma's expressions came to me then: "Everything happens for the best." It was true so often. Not *everything*, though. Not the Tragedy . . .

"Oh, Glen, have you ever seen such country!" Mrs. Folsom gasped, and as I looked out the window at the purple ridges of mountains with the sun streaking through the gigantic evergreen trees lining the road for as far as you could see, I realized what it meant to "feast your eyes" on something.

Dr. Folsom was shaking his head. "It's everything it's cracked up to be up here — the real thing. Unspoiled, virgin land that still has all the beauty of its beginning. I wonder how long it'll be before the philistines spoil it."

"Well, I'm glad we got here before they did," Mrs. Folsom replied. "And I'm glad I brought my paints along."

Dr. Folsom laughed. "You'll have enough inspiration here to keep you going for the rest of the year. Better watch out — you might evolve into a primitive."

Half the time I didn't know what they were

talking about, but it was so thrilling just to be a part of their conversations. And I kept having this feeling that with time I would learn to understand their kind of talk. It was like a completely different world from Grandma and Grandpa's.

Tommy was fast asleep with his head on my lap, and I was feeling so drowsy I just leaned my own head back. Before I dozed off I remember thinking how absolutely wonderful the air smelled. It was the pine trees, Dr. Folsom said, and I thought how much different and nicer the scent was than the kind that comes in a can.

The next thing I knew the car stopped, and as I blinked open my eyes, I saw all these pine trees and I thought we'd stopped on the road. But then I noticed a little white house with blue shutters set right inside a grove of trees, and now that my eyes were finally really open I saw a man and woman hurrying toward the car. Dr. and Mrs. Folsom were unfastening their seat belts, and Tommy raised his head slowly. When he saw we were there he started screaming with excitement and clapping his hands. He was pointing out the window, and there, just a great big hop, skip, and jump from us, was the lake, practically *yards* from the cottage. Anyway I guessed it must be the lake, because they said our cottage was on a lake. But to me it looked more like an ocean without waves. I never knew lakes were that big. I couldn't even see the end of it.

"Look at the big pool!" Tommy squealed, pointing at it. "I want to go in the pool!" Dr. Folsom laughed and lifted him high in the air, and the man and woman smiled up at him.

"You must be Dr. and Mrs. Folsom," the lady said, holding out her hand. "Welcome to Sky Cove! We're Martha and Luke Krim."

Everyone shook hands and they introduced me and Tommy, and then Dr. Folsom went to the trunk to get the luggage out while Mrs. Krim led the way up to the cottage. It seemed like from out of nowhere a tall, skinny boy appeared, and he started to help carry in the things. I brought my suitcase and Mrs. Folsom's collapsible easel and Tommy gathered some of his toys from the back seat, and we went into the cottage. There was a nice, big screened porch and then a combination kitchen-living room, and two bedrooms, and a bathroom. The walls were knotty pine, and all the windows had pretty ruffled curtains that stood up starched and clean just like Grandma's.

The furniture was old-fashioned with all flowery material, and there were hooked rugs on the floors and fancy lampshades, and everything looked clean and bright. Mrs. Krim was busy showing Mrs. Folsom where everything was in the kitchen while Mr. Krim and Derek, their son, helped Dr. Folsom put the bags in the right rooms. There were twin beds, a big dresser, and a closet in the room Tommy and I were going to share, and as I was looking the place over, I suddenly realized Tommy wasn't there. I started looking for him in the other rooms, but he wasn't in the cottage at all, so I went outside to find him. I didn't see him anywhere, so I figured he was probably back in the car, looking for the rest of his things. But he wasn't. I looked around through the trees right by the cottage, and then I heard splashing near the lake and I got a funny feeling and raced down there. And sure enough there was Tommy in the water, his hand flying around frantically. That's the last I remember. I just jumped in, shoes and all, grabbed hold of him, and then we were both out on the dock making a lake of our own, and the Folsoms and Krims were running down to us, and then we were in blankets and drinking something hot that I couldn't even taste, and Dr. and Mrs. Folsom were patting both of us and checking to make sure we were warm and dry. That's how I remember the whole thing — it all went by like a haze, everything happened so fast. It sure was a grand entrance, as Grandma would have said, and Dr. and Mrs. Folsom treated me like some kind of a goddess. And just when all the excitement started dying down, the Clintons and Lulu arrived.

Lulu came running toward me, her arms open wide and her eyes just dancing with happiness, and I burst out crying. I was so ashamed, but I couldn't help myself. She hugged me and Mrs. Folsom hugged me, and all I could think of was that if I died that very minute, it all would have been worth it.

But I was fine. So was Tommy. And for that whole week he wouldn't go near the edge of that lake unless someone was right beside him.

That someone was usually me. The Folsoms and the Clintons left me and Lulu alone with Tommy and Marcy about half of every day and all of every evening. They'd stay at the cottage every day till after lunch, and then they'd take off for sight-seeing or golf or shopping and come back in time to take us all to dinner. Evenings they'd go out again, dancing or to the movies in the nearby villages. The weather was just beautiful that week and in the mornings they'd swim and go boating, and Mrs. Folsom painted for a couple of hours every day, either in the mornings or before dinnertime. She took her sketch pad wherever she went, too, and she always looked so happy I was glad she had the chance to have such a good time with her husband. Everyone had fun, really, but no one could possibly have had the wonderful kind of time I had. It was like a dream.

Every morning when I woke up I would snuggle under the covers for a while just looking out the window that was right beside my bed. I could see the lake that was so green, and with the sun glinting on the ripples and the sky such a clear blue with fluffy clouds, it was like those paintings I always used to see at the art show that looked like copies of picture postcards. Now I could understand why artists always painted pictures like that. It was almost too beautiful to be real. But once you've been there, it's not just what you can see. It's the smells, too. Those pine trees that were right outside my window, so close I could reach out and touch them. I loved the prickly feel, but even more I loved the wonderful perfume they gave off. Every morning when I woke up and looked out the window, it was like being close to the world in a way that I had never known before. And as the day went on, each part of it had its own specialness for me.

In the mornings Lulu and I cleaned up after breakfast and at noon prepared lunches for everyone. The rest of the morning we had all to ourselves, because the Folsoms and Clintons spent that time with their children. Sometimes we took long walks in the woods and talked and talked about each of us till we felt closer than two sisters. One day Lulu confessed that she had a crush on Derek. I was surprised. I just never thought about him that way and I didn't think Lulu would either. Actually I think the only reason he hung around with us was because there weren't any boys his age there that week — just some older couples without children and two other families with little kids. There were six cottages in Sky Cove, one of them the Krims', and Derek had to help with all the chores for keeping up the cottages. But whenever he had free time he took us out in his Sailfish. I was crazy about that and he told me I was a natural, but Lulu kidded around a lot and almost tipped us over a few times.

After lunch Marcy and Tommy took naps, and that's when Lulu and I would embroider together or fix each other's hair, trying new styles and things, or fool with the makeup and nail polish Lulu had brought along. Then when the kids got up we'd go down to the lake and they'd play in the sandbox and go in the water, and sometimes Derek would take us all out for a trip around the lake in the big motorboat. For dinner we'd go into town, a five-minute drive. Often we ate at a seafood restaurant, and Lulu and I just gorged ourselves on shrimp and lobster and clam chowder. It was the first time either of us had ever tasted shellfish and we went mad for it. The Folsoms and the Clintons got the biggest kick out of watching us demolish our lobsters, especially since we got Tommy and Marcy interested in trying it, too. After dinner we'd browse around in the shops that lined the one long main street in town. The Folsoms and Clintons were always buying things. They got us some souvenirs, too, and we bought some stuff ourselves from our pay. I got a box of pine and blueberry soaps for Grandma and a pipe for Grandpa and some beautiful lures for Peter, and I had fun helping Lulu pick out presents for her family.

That was the way the week went — every day was more beautiful and wonderful than the last. It never even rained and was hardly ever cloudy. And for me it was like a whole new lifetime of experiences. Eating in restaurants was fun — I never did at home. And I'd never been in a Sailfish. In fact I'd never been in anything but an old rowboat before! But the great thing was being with the Folsoms and the Clintons in a belonging kind of way, and even better than that was being with Lulu.

The day before we were going to leave I got Tommy into his bathing suit after his nap and went over to the sandbox where Marcy and Lulu were already playing. Derek was standing there talking and laughing with Lulu, but when I came over Lulu looked at me sort of funny and Derek told her, "I'll see you down at the dock in ten minutes."

"What are you going to do?" I asked, more curious about why she looked at me so funny.

"Kitten, would you mind watching Marcy while I take a little run with Derek in the Sailfish? He asked me, being as it's about our last day and he has a little free time now. I said I couldn't possibly and leave you stuck with the kids, but he kept insisting, and I never even did say yes. I won't be mad if you say no, Kitten, honest I won't. In fact why don't *you* go with him, and *I'll* stay with the kids!"

I just looked at her. I didn't know what to say. And she went on, "Oh, now go on, I want you to have fun on your last day here!"

"But — but I don't want to go. I mean, not if you can't. And of course we can't both go. No, Lulu, you go. He asked you and I know how you feel about him. I want *you* to have fun on your last day here!" I loved going out on the Sailfish, but not without Lulu. It wouldn't have been special just to go with Derek. But I realized it was for Lulu, and I tried harder than I'd ever tried in my whole life not to show how disappointed I was. So that when she opened her mouth I wouldn't let her talk and said to her instead, "No, I just won't argue with you about it, Lulu. You know I'm always honest with you. *You* go and I won't hear any more about it. Look, he's down there waiting for you already."

She pouted unhappily, reaching over to hug me. "Well, all right, Kitten, if you insist, but I do feel bad — "

I gave her a little push, smiling. "Hurry up or he'll go without you."

She turned and waved just before she got in and I called, "Have fun!"

I watched them push off, trying not to feel left out. But I knew if it had been *me*, I wouldn't put some boy I'd probably never see again above our friendship . . . or would I? No, I wouldn't.

They were gone for about an hour. I played with the kids and kept them happy, but I felt like crawling into a hole, and when they came back, all laughing and splotched with water, I tried to act gay and as though nothing special had happened. Lulu ran up to the cottage to change and Derek paused on his way, saying, "I'm sorry you couldn't come, Kitten. Maybe I can sandwich in a little time before you leave tomorrow."

"Oh, that's okay, Derek. I guess we'll be pretty busy."

"Yeah, that's what Lulu said. When I was looking for you after lunch to ask you to go, she told me you wouldn't be allowed to — that Mrs. Folsom didn't want you to leave Tommy ever, because of that first day he fell in the lake. That's why I asked Lulu. Boy, that Mrs. Folsom sure is funny! D'you think she'd let you come with me tomorrow before you leave? You were doing so great with the Sailfish I wanted to give you one last try at it. All Lulu does is giggle, or scream when it tips too far."

It felt as though I'd been standing there with my mouth wide open for about an hour, but I guess it was only about a second and he didn't seem to notice that I had just had the biggest shock of my life. I felt all hot and cold at the same time, and as I started to mumble some kind of an answer, his name rang through the air in shrill blasts.

"Oops, I gotta run! Trash collection. See you later, Kitten."

7

Did you ever feel as if you were living in a daze? That even though you walked and talked and ate and did the things you were supposed to do, it was only your body doing them? Even, sometimes, part of your mind . . . but never, at any time, your soul? Well, that was the way I felt from that moment on until we were driving down through the winding mountains of Maine, heading for the super-highway that would give our stomachs smooth sailing for the rest of the long trip home. The other part of my mind and all of my soul really didn't start coming back to my body till we stopped at a Howard Johnson's somewhere around Boston. By then I had had plenty of hours to think, because Tommy had long ago dozed off, and Dr. and Mrs. Folsom talked together and listened to the radio. First thing in the morning they had asked me how I felt and Dr. Folsom looked at me with that doctory stare, and every once in a while they'd turn around and ask me how I was, and after I kept saying, "Fine," they finally stopped.

They had arranged to meet the Clintons at the Howard Johnson's, and I dreaded having to face Lulu more than anything in the whole world. I had made it my business not to be with her ever since Derek had dropped his little bomb. I played with Tommy in the water for the rest of that afternoon and arranged it so that he was hanging on me all the time and I had to give him my full attention. And in that way Lulu and I just didn't have a chance to talk, because Marcy started doing the same thing to her.

At dinner the night before we left, we were all seated at one big table together in the restaurant instead of me and Lulu and the kids at a separate table, the way we usually did it. Not that I could even eat. They kept asking me what was the matter, because I just picked at my food, and I said I didn't feel so very well, and when we got back to the cottage, Dr. Folsom started looking into my throat and ears, asking if anything hurt me or was my stomach upset. Then he said everything looked all right and that I was probably just tired from the big week and should go to bed early.

"We're getting an early start tomorrow anyway. We're not going out tonight, and we'll all go to bed early."

I couldn't have had better news, because I really just wanted to crawl into bed and stay there. I thought how nice it was that they were so interested in how I felt and all. Then I heard Mrs. Folsom say, "I sure hope she's not coming down with something. That's all we need!"

"Don't be such a worrywart," Dr. Folsom told her. "She's fine — just tired. Even if she is coming down with something, she'll probably hold out till we get home. I hope."

Mrs. Folsom gave a little groan. "Oh, so do I! Heavens, can you imagine that trip home with a sick kid? It would be worse than if Tommy were sick. At least he belongs to us!"

The words were so hurtful. I wished I'd never heard them. I closed my eyes, wanting desperately now to be with my Family once again. They were the only really true friends I had, the only people who *really* cared about me and would do anything in the world for me. I cried softly into my pillow so no one could hear. But instead of walking into the world of my Family, my stubborn mind could only go over and over what had happened that afternoon between me and Lulu and Derek. Just before I fell asleep I got this thought that maybe Derek had lied. *But why would he?* And I hated myself for being too chicken to tell Lulu I knew what had happened. And to tell her how I felt about her and her so-called friendship.

But it wasn't being chicken — that's what I realized during that long, nauseating drive down my beautiful mountainside. It was just not wanting to have it out with Lulu and lose the nicest friend I'd ever had in my life. I kept fighting with the idea of overlooking it — after all, I argued to myself, I'd never even known anyone like Lulu. It's true I hadn't known her for a long time, but time doesn't always matter in friendships. Still, how much did it really mean, her caring about me the way I thought she did, when she traded it all for an hour of fun with some boy? It would be the last thing in the world I'd ever think of doing to her. I wouldn't lie to her for anyone, not even my own family — or Family.

"Well, they beat us here!" Dr. Folsom said as he swung the car into a parking space in the restaurant lot. The Clintons were just ready to go inside when Dr. Clinton spotted us and started waving, and we could hardly hold Tommy back when he caught sight of Marcy. Everyone was babbling at once, except me and Lulu, but they didn't notice that. I tried not to have to look at her, but she waited for me, and when the others walked inside, I couldn't avoid her any longer.

"Well, hi, Kitten! Aren't you glad to see me?" Her voice was so warm that I couldn't help smiling. It seemed years since I'd done it last. "Now, that's better. Don't worry, your face won't crack!"

I laughed and she did too. She had a tinkly laugh that I always loved. "For a while there I thought you were mad at me! Why, it looked like you were avoiding me. I thought maybe you really *were* mad that I went with Derek after all."

I took a deep breath. "I wasn't, Lulu. Not till Derek told me afterward that he was going to ask *me* — and you told him I couldn't go."

She turned pale and the smile froze on her face. *"He said that?"*

I nodded. "That's why he asked you, he said. I really wouldn't have cared, Lulu. That old boat ride didn't mean anything to *me*. But the way you lied about the whole thing . . ."

"Kitten! Kitten!" Tommy had burst out the door and was tugging at my arm. "Come, come! Lulu" — and he grabbed at her arm with his other hand — "you both come too."

She glared at me now and there was no longer sunlight dancing in her eyes. "If that's what you want to think, then go ahead." She tossed her head and opened the door and just ran inside. I followed with Tommy and took the seat left for me between him and Marcy at the big round table where everyone was already seated. Lulu pouted into her menu and I made a point of not looking in her direction. Between the adults chattering and the kids babbling, no one even noticed that Lulu and I neither spoke — nor ate. And the last half of the trip home was even more miserable than the first.

The only lucky thing was that Peter got home about a half hour before me! It couldn't have worked out better, because I couldn't possibly tell Grandma and Grandpa what had

happened between me and Lulu, and by now
the whole wonderful fun part of the week had
been swallowed up by that. I knew I must be
the unhappiest kid alive.

Peter was just the opposite. He was going
strong about his weekend, minute by minute,
and when I got in, he was into Saturday afternoon. I'd come just in time to hear about the
greatest catch that was ever landed on the
North American coast, by none other than
Peter Tate and Charlie Korn. Honestly, he
was just about busting up with excitement,
and Grandma and Grandpa were all smiles.
They tried to stop him for a little intermis-
sion when I came in, fussing over me and
asking me how everything was. It was easy
to fake it, because it was a happy feeling to
see them again, and so nice and comfortable
to be back home after all that traveling. They
looked like they wanted to eat me up and that
started me feeling better, so that when they
asked how everything was, I told them great
and wonderful. And as I told them little
things, all the nice parts till the end kept coming back, and they must have seen that I really
seemed as happy as I said. They kept oohing
and ahing about how healthy I looked and how
healthy Peter looked and who was tanner and

did we eat well — why, hadn't we gained some weight! But soon they gave their attention back to Peter. They had to, he just wouldn't stop talking.

It was really a pretty funny sight. We were all in the living room, Grandma and Grandpa seated on the sofa and Peter standing in the middle of the room, waving his arms around while he talked, his suitcase open on the floor in front of him and things spilling out all over it, as every couple of minutes he'd dive down and dig out something else he wanted to show us. There was a separate ditty bag of all the dirty clothes and precious collections — shells, rocks, and pieces of colored glass — and of course his fishing stuff was out on the porch.

Grandpa and Grandma's faces just absolutely shone as they listened to Peter and every once in a while glanced at me, and then they'd smile at each other with such happiness that my own terrible, raw feelings started to soften up. They beckoned for me to come sit between them, and when I did they both put their arms around me, and I felt nice and safe and glad to be back with the people who loved me, even though they didn't make a big thing of showing it a whole lot or using fancy words about it. It struck me then, I guess, because this was the first time I'd ever been away from home. Grandma and Grandpa were plain people, but the joy and pride that they beamed out at us now, for me and Peter, would have matched any of the fanciest, most sophisticated parents.

" — And we reeled it in and reeled it in," Peter's voice droned on as he stood gazing at us now, looking almost hypnotized, "and it was putting up one heck of a struggle. We knew it was a biggie. Even Mr. Korn was all excited, because this one had to be a winner. Well, it suddenly came flapping up and all around and we got it into the boat, and by now everyone on the whole fishing boat was crowding around, and what do you think it was?"

"An eel," I said.

"Oh, yeah, Miss Smarty-pants?" Grandpa said, grinning till it seemed he was going to burst. "Tell her, Peter." Obviously they had already heard all about it.

"Would you believe a thirty-eight-inch blue?"

"Blue what?" I said.

"Blue*fish*!" Peter screamed. "How dumb can you get?"

"Really? Honest? Thirty-eight inches? Are you sure?"

Peter nodded gleefully. "Man, wow, you should have seen the excitement on that boat! Me and Charlie were heroes!" His face was really lit up now. "Want me to prove it? Grandpa, where's that certificate I gave you?"

Grandpa took a folded paper out of his shirt pocket. "Right here, son. I'm going to show it to the men at work tomorrow. Cast your eyes on this, you little doubting Thomas," he said as he handed me a printed paper with Peter's and Charlie's names written in, showing they'd caught a thirty-eight-inch bluefish the day before!

"Hey, wow, that's great!" I said, and Peter just kept grinning at me. "But — where's the fish?" I jumped up. "Is it on the back porch?"

Grandma pulled me back, laughing. "No, come back."

Peter pouted now. "We wanted to bring it home alive, or at least frozen in one piece, but on the boat they said we couldn't. It didn't fit in the freezer. They cleaned it and cut it all up and froze it, and we brought it back in the ice chest. But we have lots of pictures of it. Mr. Korn took a whole roll of film of the fish and us holding it. He's going to have it developed tomorrow at one of those quick places and he's going to have copies made for me and Charlie and him. Then you'll see for yourself!"

I smiled at him. "I believe you, Peter. I should have known all along what a great fisherman you are! But, hey, where are the cut-up pieces of fish? Are we going to eat it?"

"I should say so," Grandma said.

"Mr. Korn took it all home. He's going to bring mine over tomorrow. Man, we'll have fish for the rest of the summer! Can I give some to Alfie? Wait'll I tell him about it — and Skint!" Suddenly he turned to me. "Hey, how was your vacation? Did you and Lulu have fun? Did anyone go fishing?"

My heart sort of dropped, but I laughed. "That's about the only thing we didn't do. But we went boating a lot, and I learned how to sail a Sailfish. And we went to a terrific restaurant and had lobster and shrimp and clam chowder — "

"Hey, so did we! We had quahog chowder, that white stuff. It was great!"

"Yes, they said it's New England style or something. Grandma, can you make it for us? How did you like the lobster, Peter?"

"Was it *good*, but it sure was a mess of trouble to eat!"

"Oh, I just remembered!" I ran over and opened my suitcase to find the presents. "Here," I said, handing them out. "Some special souvenirs from Maine."

You'd think I'd given them solid gold things the way they acted. Grandma and Grandpa kissed me, and Peter looked like he wanted to when he saw those lures.

"Well," Grandpa said as we gathered all our things and prepared to go upstairs — it was very late and we were both pretty tired by now — "we're pleased you children had such a good time. We missed you and we're glad you're both back safe and sound. Now that you've had a chance to see a little bit more of the world — well — " He shrugged and looked at Grandma sort of helplessly and she chimed in, "Every bird likes his own nest best."

Peter and I both smiled and told them good night, and as I snuggled down into my wonderful very own bed, I wondered if Peter thought the same thing: that maybe Grandma and Grandpa and all their sayings were right after all.

But the moment I woke up the next morning, I was very depressed. I mean, really depressed. I wanted to cry when I looked out the window and saw the ugly old house across the way with its shack of a garage and the cement sidewalk shining in the sunlight. I longed for the beautiful blue Maine sky and my beloved lake that I'd been able to see from my window when I awoke every morning. And that wonderful smell of the pine trees. And the soft breezes, and the warm wooden dock, the boats, and the people, and being part of it all. . . . And Lulu every day, and each day something different to do, to talk about.

I walked over to the Folsoms' very slowly. Peter was still sleeping when I left, and Grandpa had long ago gone to work, so Grandma sat with me at breakfast and asked me two thousand questions about every single thing we did and said. Of course I didn't tell her about Lulu at the end. I decided I just wasn't going to talk about it to anyone. It would have to come out sooner or later, especially since Peter was friendly with Alfie now. But I would just let it come out in its own time. Right now it still felt like a raw wound, and I didn't want to go near it. I promised myself I wouldn't even think about it. Except I did, about every minute.

But as soon as I got to the Folsoms' I didn't

have any more time to think about myself. Mrs. Folsom was all excited and she hugged me when I came in. It was funny — a few weeks ago that would have been the high point of my day. But now I knew that it meant nothing — it was like another person saying hello.

"Kitten, the most wonderful news! The art show has accepted all my paintings — the letter came while we were away — and I have to go today to be assigned my spot and get all the rest of the instructions. Goodness, I'm not even all unpacked yet and the show starts tomorrow. Do you think you could help me, hon? Just my luck, Claire can' come today."

"Of course. I'd love to!"

"Oh, you're a darling!" She gave me another quick squeeze. "Look, Tommy's things are all up in his room, but I didn't have a moment to sort them. Would you be a sweetheart and do it? Put all the soiled clothing in the hamper and sort out his toys. You know where everything goes. There's a separate section with all the clean stuff. You can just put it away. Then if you'd be a real dear, during his naptime if you'd just put our golf clubs and air mattresses and sneakers and

115

things like that away in the garage and basement, I'll be indebted to you for life."

She left in a little while and Tommy kept me busy following him in and out of the house. It seemed like he wanted to play with every single one of his toys that he hadn't seen in a week, and it was easier for me to put them back afterward than to get him to do it. When he was ready for his nap, I was readier for one, but I had to do all those things Mrs. Folsom asked me to, and by the time I finished, he was up again and ready for action. I managed to talk him into going in the pool, and even though he kept me busy all the time, it was easier than the morning's routine. I couldn't wait till the afternoon was over, and as soon as Mrs. Folsom got home, all fluttery with excitement about the prime spot she had for the show and everyone she had met, I got away as fast as I could.

When I got home, our back porch looked like a day camp. Skint, Alfie, two other boys from down the block, and another kid I'd never even seen before were all sitting around with Peter and Charlie listening to the great tale of the Big Catch and passing around the snapshots that Charlie had brought over for Peter. I really could hardly believe it when I saw them.

116

I mean, hearing about a thirty-eight-inch fish is one thing, but seeing it is something else. There were pictures of Peter and Charlie holding it, and that's how you could really see how big it was. It was gigantic!

"My father's taking some of the pictures over to the newspaper," Charlie told me, and Peter took me in to the freezer to show me the fish steaks in their neat transparent wrappings. Alfie came in after us, but I couldn't bear the sight of him and I hurried up to my room and flopped on the bed, and Grandpa had to shake me to wake me up for dinner.

They were worried that I was coming down with something. I wanted to tell them that I *was* down with something: a great big case of heartbreak. Now that I was back home it was even worse, because before we went to Maine, Lulu and I had started spending all our time together. She was the only person in the whole world who knew my deepest secrets, and I hers. And now we weren't even talking!

I explained to Grandma and Grandpa that I was still tired from the trip, and they didn't have to convince me to go to bed early. Grandma wanted me to stay home from work the next day, but that would have been the worst thing to do. I'd just have more time to think about how miserable I was. Besides, Mrs. Folsom was counting on me to come especially, because it was the first day of the art show and she needed me to be with Tommy. When I explained that to Grandma, she argued, "But I don't want you getting sick, child. You look so peaked. Remember, 'life is not merely being alive, but being well.' You must promise to come home if you're not feeling up to it. You can bring Tommy with you if Claire isn't there. And don't go in the pool today."

"I promise." It happened to be a beautiful day anyway — bright and sunny, but not too hot, and there was a soft breeze. It was a perfect day just to sit around without going swimming, and it sure was a great day for an art show. I wished I could go, and when Mrs. Folsom asked me if I'd like to take a walk down with Tommy, I felt like hugging her.

It's funny, but on the way over what Grandma had said came back to me — about life isn't only being alive but being healthy. I thought, it's being *happy*. Otherwise what was the point? I wasn't even concerned about the possibility that someone I knew might run into Mrs. Folsom. At that moment it just didn't seem to matter.

118

The art show was really busy. I saw lots of my friends from school there, and they all crowded around Tommy and made a big fuss over him and he loved every minute. It was fun looking at the jewelry stands and the sculpture, and of course, all the paintings and drawings. Tommy loved the clowns that were painted on velvet, and when we got to Mrs. Folsom's exhibit, he just went wild to see her, and she took him around to show him off to everyone. I couldn't wait to see my painting. I was kind of nervous about it and prayed no one would be looking at it while I was. No one was, and I could just stand there and stare. I could hardly believe it, how beautiful it looked. It was sort of like a mosaic of all pretty colors, and you had to look awhile before it took any kind of form, and with the sun so bright the colors looked changed, too.

"How does it look?" Mrs. Folsom was smiling at me, and I smiled back.

"Beautiful! It really does! I didn't think — " I stopped, realizing I didn't want to say what I thought.

She laughed. "I know, neither did I. But I'm more pleased with it than ever. The people who have come by seemed to like it, but it's been pretty quiet so far. Things will pick up this evening. Oh, Kitten, when it's time for you to leave, would you take Tommy over to the Clintons'? Paula's going to keep him for me till I get home."

I nodded numbly. *I would see Lulu.* What would I say? What would she do?

My heart pounded as we went up the walk. But Mrs. Clinton called to us from the patio. "We're over here, Kitten." I was trembling by the time we got there, but she was alone with Marcy, who was coloring in a book on the grass. "Lulu left early — she didn't feel so well. How are you, Kitten?"

"Fine." I smiled my brightest.

"Oh, I'm glad. I think both you girls looked a little peaked when we came back. I guess it was vacationitis." She smiled warmly and I wished with all my heart that I could pour out my misery to her. I don't know what gave me that crazy thought, because I certainly didn't know Mrs. Clinton very well. She was a much quieter type than Mrs. Folsom, and though of course I saw her a lot, especially in Maine when we were all together so much, I never had any kind of important talks with her. But she had this sincere way about her. Lulu always told me how she would ask her about herself and her family and that she really cared. Now, since that week in Maine, she just seemed like an old friend, and I had the funny feeling she would understand. At least be interested. But I couldn't say a word.

"Would you like some lemonade, dear?"

Maybe if we sat around together for a while, I could get up my courage. But I didn't even have the chance to answer before the phone rang. She jumped up. "Why don't you just pour yourself a glass of lemonade?"

"Thank you very much, but I really have to go home." I watched her run into the house, wishing the phone had waited just ten minutes to ring — and then glad it hadn't. Because I probably would have spilled out everything about me and Lulu and then I'd be sorry afterward.

That night I was even more tired than the day before, though I hadn't worked half as hard. *What's the matter with me?* I hugged my pillow. *Maybe I am coming down with something.* I dreamt the phone was ringing and that it was Lulu and she wanted to make up with me. And then I was awake and the phone *was* ringing. My heart really pounded.

I thought it was the middle of the night and that my clock had stopped because it said eight-thirty. But then when I saw the lights on downstairs, I realized it hadn't and remembered I'd gone to bed early again.

"Yessir," Grandpa was saying over the phone, "that's my grandson, all right. How do you like that . . ."

Peter's fish story! Man, the kid was really getting to be a celebrity. Little did I know. It turned out to be a reporter from our local paper calling, and sure enough, a big picture of Peter and Charlie holding that enormous fish was in the paper the next day.

8

Tommy and I were outside the next afternoon
when the Folsoms' paperboy came. He passed
by while I was pushing Tommy on the swing,
and when he gave me their paper, I just laid
it on the patio chaise. I'd have forgotten about
it if Tommy hadn't asked me to read him the
comics when he spied it there. I'd done that
once when I couldn't think of anything else
to do with him, and since then whenever he
saw the newspaper he begged me to read him
the comics. And there, right below "Nancy"
on the bottom of the page, was a great big
picture of Peter and Charlie with the whole
story: "Peter Tate, nine, grandson of Mr. and

Mrs. Thomas Herbert, 72 Vale Road . . ." and it told about how they'd caught this monster fish. My hand started shaking until I realized that even if Mrs. Folsom did see it — and she probably wouldn't, she was so busy with the art show — she still wouldn't have any way of knowing he was my brother. After all anyone's name could be Tate, and she probably didn't even remember the name of my street. But what if she did — what if she asked me about it. . . . *Why did Peter have to be such a celebrity!* Oh, well, I thought then, Mrs. Folsom certainly doesn't read the comics, and if she just happened to, why would she be interested in a picture of some kids with a fish? But just in case, I decided, I'd just say he was my cousin. I planned my explanation while I was waiting for Jeannie and Ann to pick me up to go to the art show.

The three of us had gone to the art show together for the last two years, so it was like a standing date by now. That was the nice thing about having old friends: you could always go back to them when you needed to. I hadn't seen much of Jeannie and Ann lately, not till after I got back from Maine and wasn't friends with Lulu anymore. I started going over to their houses after supper the way I used to, and they loved hearing about my trip and what it was like in Maine.

"Hey, where's the star of the family?" Jeannie said when I opened the door for her and Ann.

I thought for a moment, then said, "Oh, Peter! Isn't that a great picture?"

Ann giggled. "How're you going to live with him now?"

I groaned. "It's not going to be easy."

"Where is he?"

"At the art show. They left already, he and my grandparents."

"Let's get going," Ann said. "We don't want to miss anything."

"How's that girl Lulu?" Jeannie asked me as we walked on down the street. "We haven't seen you around with her since you got back from Maine."

"Oh, she's fine," I said quickly. "She's been pretty busy." I changed the subject as fast as I could. "Do you know what Tommy tried to do today? He wanted to go in the pool with his overalls on — and his sneakers!"

Ann clutched her head. "You must have your hands full with him! Listen, are you still so crazy about that job, Kitten? Aren't you awful sick of that spoiled brat by now?"

"No, I love Tommy!"

Jeannie and Ann exchanged a funny look. "And what about Mrs. Folsom?" Jeannie said. "Are you still in love with her, too?"

"I don't know what you have against her!" I snapped back. "Just because your cousin doesn't like her — and I know people talk about her. But she's been real wonderful to me. Yes, I still like her." Of course it wasn't true. I didn't like her the same way I did at the beginning, but I'd never tell that to them.

That night was the biggest time of the art show. A band played, and some teen-age groups sang, and there were refreshment stands — it was more like a carnival. Cotton candy stuck to everything, and sometimes people would start dancing around right in the street. We kept running into Grandma and Grandpa and Peter, and every time someone else was stopping them to congratulate them about the fish. Once I saw Arletta with a bunch of her friends and she gave me a big hello, and right after that who did I see but Steve and a friend of his! I prayed I'd see Lulu — I honestly did! I had it all planned that I'd just look right past her, as though I didn't even see her. Then sometimes I'd think, well, maybe I'd change my mind at the last minute and decide to say "hi" as though nothing had happened. And then I saw her.

I just looked up while I was unwrapping a piece of bubble gum, and she was standing there staring at me, and it was like a dream. She had this funny look on her face, and before I could decide just what I was going to do, she said in this sort of frantic voice, "Kitten, have you seen Alfie? I've lost him, and he has all our money to keep — " She looked like she was going to burst out crying, and then suddenly we heard someone screeching, "Lulu — *Lulu!* I'm over here!" She spun around and zipped off in the direction of Alfie's voice, and that was the last I saw of her.

It was right afterward that I met Mrs. Folsom. She was standing around with another man and woman, and she called me over and introduced me. Jeannie and Ann were talking to some girls from down the block we'd just met. I had to be thankful for that, because Mrs. Folsom said, "Kitten, someone showed me today's paper with a picture of a boy by the name of Peter Tate, who caught a gigantic fish. Don't you live on Vale Road? It said — "

"Oh, yes, that's my cousin. He came down with my grandparents. His dad and mine are brothers." I kept my fingers crossed, glad I had planned for it.

"Oh, I was wondering. Because I knew you didn't have a brother that age, and when I saw the name and the same street . . ." Someone called to her then, and I clenched my fists to hide my shaking hands.

I'm sure I wouldn't have had to worry — I know she'd have forgotten about it if nothing else unusual had happened. I would have worked for her the next three weeks, then the summer would have been over and I'd have gone back to school, and we'd have forgotten about each other as the years went by. I hate to admit it, but I can't help thinking of Grandma and Grandpa's dumb old sayings again. Especially the one that might tell this story: "Man proposes, God disposes."

The thing that caused all the trouble was that Mrs. Folsom won first prize in the art show for her painting called "Young Girl." That was my portrait. The judging was done the next morning, and when it was over, Mrs. Folsom had to come home to recover. While she was telling Tommy and me about it, she looked like the most beautiful creature on the earth. She called up her husband then, and she was so happy she was almost crying. And as I watched her, and listened to her, I really understood what had made me tell her all those stories when I first met her, about my Family being my family. I guess I knew it was wrong, just as much as I knew I couldn't stop myself.

The doorbell rang as Mrs. Folsom hung up the phone, and she went to get it while I chased after Tommy who was screaming in his room. He had pulled down a carton of toys from his closet shelf, and they all came piling on top of him. After I kissed each booboo, we made a game of picking everything up and putting it back, and then I had to talk him into not doing it again. Next was story and naptime, and he fell asleep in the middle of the second page. As I drew his curtains, Mrs. Folsom tiptoed in, kissed his cheek, and beckoned me to follow her downstairs.

"There's someone here who wants to meet you," she told me as she pointed to the living room, where a little fat lady with dyed blond hair and a camera around her neck stood grinning at me.

"*Well!*" The word was more like a sharp breath. "So this is the subject! How absolutely charming!"

"Kitten, this is Mrs. Medley, a reporter for

the local paper. She came to interview me because of the prize."

"*Kitten!* And what is your real name, dear?"

"Carol Ann." For some reason I didn't understand then, I had a funny feeling, all tied up with wishing I could escape.

"Carol Ann Tate," Mrs. Folsom supplied. "Her initials spell CAT — that's how she came by her nickname."

"Why, that's precious! Hmm, *Tate.* You aren't related to that little boy who caught the big fish, are you?" As I nodded dumbly she said, "Well, what a coincidence! I did that story for the paper just the day before yesterday! He and his little friend came down to the office with the father, and I did the interview. They wanted us to use the picture they'd taken of them with the fish, though. Poor little tyke, the other lad's father told me he's an orphan, lives with his grandparents and sis — uh, how did you say you're related to him, dear?" She had pulled out a notebook and begun writing. When I stared at her blankly, she said, "What a stroke of luck to find the subject of the portrait right here with you, Mrs. Folsom! I'd love to do a little interview

130

with you, dear, and take some pictures. Would that be all right?"

I looked at Mrs. Folsom with this helpless feeling. She was all smiles. "Oh, go ahead, Kitten! Don't be bashful. Your family will be thrilled."

"Now" — and she was scribbling away — "they call you Kitten, do they? And don't tell me you're the fisherman's sister!"

I nodded. It would be in the paper. How could I possibly go on with my stories? I didn't look at Mrs. Folsom but stared at the lady's white beads.

"Well, what a coincidence! This will be a real gem of a story! Now, let's get your address first and the name of your par — er, that is your grandparents, is that right? You don't have any other sisters or brothers, do you?" I shook my head, then noticed Mrs. Folsom leaving the room. I bit my lips as she kept asking me all these dumb questions, like my school and my grade, and if I had any special interest in art, and about my baby-sitting job, and what I thought of the painting. I started feeling a little sick by the time it was all over, and as she thanked me and Mrs. Folsom, who had come back into the room when it was all over, I felt as though

I had left the earth and that just my body had stayed. Everyone's voice seemed to be coming from far away, even after the reporter left and Mrs. Folsom asked me to come in the kitchen and sit down. She poured me a glass of soda, but I just stared at it. I wanted to jump up and run out of her house and never come near it, or her, again.

"Do you have something to tell me, Kitten?"

I shrugged. "I guess not."

"But you must have *something* to say. I mean, is it true, all those things you told that woman about your family?"

I nodded.

"And that boy who was in the paper *is* your brother, not your cousin, as you told me at the art show last night?"

I nodded again.

"So all those other people you told me about are just — made up?"

Her voice was still coming from a long way off. I nodded again. I wanted more than anything in the whole world to explain everything, the reason I had told her all those things, but I knew that if I tried to say a word I'd burst out crying.

Suddenly she raised her voice. "Kitten — *if that's really your name* — don't you have any explanation? Is that all you can do — nod your head? After telling me all those lies? What am I supposed to tell my husband?"

How could I tell her they weren't really lies? I looked at her, all ready to try — I really was. But the look on her face stopped me. She was staring right through me, and I knew then that she'd never be the least bit interested either in my reasons or in me. I opened my mouth and nothing would come out. I finally managed to say, "I'm really awful sorry. I have to go home." And I ran out the door.

This time I didn't only feel sick — I really was. I never could figure out if the awful virus I had would have happened anyway or if it got hold of me because I was just so low. And let me tell you, I never felt lower in my life. I had cut myself off from Lulu and shamed myself before Mrs. Folsom, two of the most important people in my life. Of course, with Lulu it was different; it was a point of honor. But, still, now I had no one who was special anymore, and nothing but this terrible virus that made me feel every minute of the next twenty-four hours that I wanted to die.

Grandma and Grandpa were so nice to me, and even Peter tried to help, but I couldn't eat a thing and I didn't want to talk to anyone. Grandma kept bringing tea and juice and said I had to drink something, but I couldn't keep a thing down anyway. One minute I was boiling and the next freezing, and I kept falling asleep, waking only long enough to be sick. When Grandma and Peter came up with the newspaper the next afternoon with the story about Mrs. Folsom and me in it, I didn't even want to look at it, and they thought it was because I was so sick. Little did they know that it made me even sicker! Peter was all excited, especially when he saw his name mentioned again, and Grandma was thrilled, just like Mrs. Folsom said she'd be. She couldn't wait for Grandpa to come home to show it to him, and he patted my hair back and told them to leave me be until I felt better.

It was around that time that I realized I was beginning to feel a little better. I wasn't feeling sick anymore, just awfully weak and hungry. Grandma gave me some Jell-O, and after I ate half I was full. Grandpa was just taking the dish away when the doorbell rang, and I heard Grandma at the door, saying in her special company voice, "Why, how do you do, Mrs. Folsom! Please come in. It's such a pleasure to meet you."

At first I couldn't believe my ears. I crawled under the covers. But when I was there awhile and didn't hear a sound, I came back out, deciding that when I heard them coming up I'd just pretend I was asleep. Then I heard the conversation from below. The living room was right at the bottom of the stairs and my room was at the top. It was almost like being in the same room.

" — so sorry to hear that Kitten is sick," I heard Mrs. Folsom saying now. "When you called I had Tommy in the tub. So instead of calling back I thought I'd just stop by and say hello. I wanted to leave Kitten's money, too."

"Well, now, that was entirely unnecessary," Grandma said, "but I am glad you came so we have the chance to meet. Kitten has talked about you so much, and she had such a lovely time on the trip. And she's just wild about your little boy."

"Tommy feels the same about her. She's a very capable and charming little girl. I must say I'm glad to have the chance to meet you both at last, too. I'm afraid it's long overdue. I suppose I should have paid this call a long time ago, and then maybe — " She stopped and I strained my ears, wondering if they were whispering something. Then I heard

Grandpa, "Is there something wrong, Mrs. Folsom?"

"Well, not exactly. I — uh — well, I don't know just how to say this."

"What is it?" Grandma demanded, sounding so afraid.

"Well, you do know, don't you, that Kitten won't be coming back to work for me?"

There was a short silence and then Grandpa said, "No, we knew nothing about that. Will you please tell us what's the trouble, Mrs. Folsom?"

"Has she told you anything at all since she left my house yesterday?"

"No," Grandma replied. "When she got home she was feeling sick, and I put her to bed and gave her a hotwater bottle and some tea. But she didn't say anything about the day — nothing at all. Just how sick she was. Poor child, she hasn't been this sick since she had the flu three years ago. But tell us, please . . ."

"Well, yesterday when that reporter came to interview me and asked who the subject of my painting was and I told her that she was at my house, she asked to meet her. Not till then, when she started answering this reporter's questions, did I find out that everything

136

Kitten had told me about her family wasn't true."

"Wasn't true?" Grandpa repeated, as though he hadn't heard her right.

"Yes. You see — "

At that point I wanted to crawl back under the covers, but I wouldn't let myself. This time I made myself suffer through the whole thing. Mrs. Folsom told them from the beginning, from the time we'd met in Mayo's, all about my Family, and then the story of Peter's picture in the paper. How before we left Maine I would relay messages back and forth, and the tale I told about my grandparents coming down to stay with us.

"Mrs. Folsom," Grandma said when she'd finished her story, "how has this hurt you?"

"What do you mean?"

"Have the — stories Kitten told you hurt you or your husband or child in any way?"

"Why, of course not! I don't understand — "

"Well, then *I* don't understand why you're making such a serious thing of it. We're certainly sorry Kitten told you all these little tales, but I don't see any harm they did to anyone."

"Do you mean that you don't care if your

granddaughter goes around telling these terrible lies? That it doesn't bother you?"

"Yes," Grandpa spoke up now, "it does bother us. It is a pity that the poor child craves a more normal kind of family so much that she has to dream one up. We certainly never knew about this, you can be sure. I can't explain it any better than to say that it was — well, like they say, *wishful thinking*."

"Well, of course I understand. But aren't you more concerned than that? Don't you realize that she may be terribly — sick?"

"Yes," Grandma said now in that real firm voice of hers, "she is terribly sick. She's got one of these twenty-four-hour viruses. That's what Dr. Delby calls it. And we're nursing her back to good health, and she's getting better and will probably be fine tomorrow. But that's the only kind of sick she is, Mrs. Folsom."

Mrs. Folsom gave one of her pretty little laughs. "Well, yes, I know that, Mrs. Herbert, but that isn't what I meant. Now look, I came here to you as a friend of Kitten's. Someone who cares about her and wants to help her. She's a lovely, bright little youngster, but we don't think she should be around Tommy anymore. As my husband said, she may get worse — you know, if you let these things go too long, it's much harder to deal with them. She's still only a child, and with the proper psychiatric treatment you'll be surprised how quickly she can be helped. You must understand . . ."

I had gone ice cold. What was she saying? Was it true? Would Grandma and Grandpa believe her? She said *her husband said.* He's a doctor! Surely they wouldn't refuse to believe a doctor. *The proper psychiatric treatment* . . . Does that mean going to a mental hospital? My hands were numb as they clutched the blankets. I was afraid to listen anymore, but now I heard Grandma's voice. It sounded like it did when Peter walked across the living room carpet with muddy sneakers.

"Mrs. Folsom, my husband and I are grateful that you came by to see how Kitten is, and we thank you for everything that needs thanking. Now, we're not educated people, and with all due respect to you and your husband I just can't think along those lines, and you can't persuade me that anything you've said about Kitten is right. Now, I don't say that psychiatric help isn't important for certain people at certain times, but in this case I'm afraid you're way off the mark. Our granddaughter has every good reason to dream herself up a glamorous family to make up for what she lost out on, and though I'm not a doctor or anything near it, I'm willing to wager that it's just a phase in her life right now and that she'll outgrow it."

"And you, Mr. Herbert?" Mrs. Folsom said. "Is that what you think, too?"

"I can't hold with any of this psychiatric business, not in this case. What our Kitten needs is people who love her and care about her, the way you said you do. But not that you really do. Because if you did, you would have made it your business to meet us a long time ago."

My mouth dropped open. I had never heard Grandma or Grandpa speak to a stranger like that.

"Well, I can see I made a big mistake." Mrs. Folsom's voice was angry now, too. "I had only the best of intentions when I came here. I thought you would want to know these things about Kitten. When a child goes around telling such terrible lies — "

"Terrible lies?" Grandpa's voice wasn't angry now, but very calm. "You know, Mrs. Folsom, I learned a poem once when I was a young chap, and there are three lines I never forgot:

But I, being poor, have only my dreams;
I have spread my dreams under your feet;
Tread softly because you tread on my dreams.

"I was a big dreamer when I was a lad, too. Poor, the way people were poor then, and those lines meant a lot to me. Kitten is poor in another way, she and her brother. And she must have been feeling it more than we ever knew. You're very young, Mrs. Folsom, and you're very wrapped up in yourself. Otherwise you'd understand that the things Kitten told you weren't terrible lies, but simply her poor dreams that she was spreading under your feet. You must learn to tread more softly."

I didn't listen anymore. I didn't want to hear Mrs. Folsom say anything else. I closed my eyes and in the next moment I heard the front door open and close. She was gone. I kept my eyes closed as Grandma and Grandpa came quietly up the steps and into my room. *Why couldn't I have died today when I felt like it?* I wondered. The idea of having to have the whole thing out with them all over again made me more miserable than ever. Sure they stuck up for me to a stranger. But it wouldn't be the same when they got me alone.

Suddenly I felt Grandma bend over and kiss me, and then I felt Grandpa's hand smoothing back my hair and patting my cheek. When they got to the doorway, Grandma whispered, "Let's never even tell her she was here."

9

Did you ever go to bed at night wishing the day hadn't happened, that it was just a bad dream, and wake up in the morning believing it? That's what it was like the next day. The sun was streaming into my room, even through the window shade, and after I opened my eyes and realized with a happy shock that I didn't feel sick anymore, I was sure I must have dreamt everything. *Everything*.

I zipped out of bed and pulled up the shade and looked out the window. It was a beautiful day and the little kids down on the sidewalk were hooking their tricycles together into a train. All of a sudden I remembered Tommy

— and my job. I looked at the clock. It was eleven! No wonder my stomach felt so absolutely empty. I was *starving*. And I was late. How could I have — But by then I knew I couldn't fool myself any longer. It hadn't been a dream, it had been a nightmare; but every minute of it had been real. And still was.

Except that Grandma and Grandpa weren't angry at me. They'd stood up for me against all those mean things Mrs. Folsom said. I'd never have thought she would have said such things about me. I thought she cared about me a little bit. Enough to trust me with her child. But now that she'd found out that I told her lies, she no longer had any use for me. Suddenly I remembered all those things people had said about her: Lulu said she was so in love with herself, and Jeannie's cousin called her a phony. But I hadn't wanted to hear those things. I had wanted her to be the way I thought she was.

I brushed my teeth furiously, feeling warmer inside when I remembered all the nice things Grandma and Grandpa had told her. I guessed then that it couldn't have been very easy for them to bring up their daughter's

children. They couldn't help it if they weren't
our mother and father.

I heard the doorbell as I was putting on
my sneakers. It sounded like one of Peter's
friends talking to Grandma. I couldn't wait
to get down to eat, and as I ran through the
living room toward the kitchen, a pink form
rose up and said in a voice that I thought must
have come from my own wild imagination,
"Kitten . . ."

I could only stare at Lulu. But then my own
voice finally worked. "Well — hi." I stood
very still and so did she.

"Kitten, I came to apologize. I've been
wanting to do it ever since Maine, and I just
didn't have the nerve. And then when I saw
the story about you in the paper yesterday, I
knew I had to come no matter what, because I
promised you . . ." Her voice trailed off as she
kept looking at me with this question in her
eyes.

"I'm glad you came, Lulu." I couldn't seem
to say very much, but so many things raced
through my mind.

"Oh, Kitten." And she still stood there so
frozen, but her voice was shaky now. "I don't
know why I pulled that nasty trick with Derek.

145

I didn't think you'd care so much, but — well, I shouldn't have lied, and you can believe me, I've been sorry ever since. Can you — would you forgive and forget, Kitten?" She held out her hand to me sort of shyly and I grasped it.

"Yes, I can, Lulu, and I do. I've missed you a lot. I'm glad you came."

"I thought this would sort of prove our friendship. Because like I said, Kitten, I promised to help you out if it ever, you know, came out with Mrs. Folsom. And from the looks of things, it has."

I smiled now. "It sure has. It's great of you, Lulu." I couldn't resist, " 'A friend in need is a friend indeed.' Right?"

She laughed. "Grandma's right again!" Then her face got real serious. "Oh, Kitten, you don't know how many times I wanted to come over and apologize. But I couldn't get myself to. I was ashamed. And so miserable."

I just stared at her. It was the kind of thing that I kept daydreaming she would say to me, every day since our fight. Now that she said it I was trying to make myself believe it was really happening.

"But really," she was going on now, "we

have to get you out of this. I took off from work today so I could help you. Now, I was thinking — "

I held up my hand. "Never mind, Lulu. It's all over with Mrs. Folsom. She found out everything."

She looked shocked. "Truly? Oh, Kitten, what are we going to do?"

"Kitten!" Grandma called from the kitchen. "Are you downstairs yet?"

"Yes, Grandma, I'm in here with Lulu."

She appeared in the doorway. "Well, good morning! I heard you getting up so I told Lulu to wait. How do you feel, dear?"

"All better. And starving!"

"Aha! 'The feeling of health is acquired only by sickness.' Well, you come on in the kitchen and we'll fix that up. Both of you." She looked at me very closely as I passed her and felt my forehead. "Your color is back. You do look better. But you must take it easy today. Get yourself a good rest. 'Rest is sweet after strife.' "

I laughed. "*Rest* — that's all I've been doing!" As Grandma walked back into the kitchen, I whispered to Lulu, "I'll tell you all about it later. It's some story!"

"You're right, that's some story," Lulu

agreed as we sat under the peach tree afterward, full of eggs and breakfast buns and proverbs. She shook her head. "I'd figured on Mrs. Folsom being upset when she found out, but I can't understand why she's so — so mad, and so mean about it. After all . . ." Suddenly she smiled one of her impish grins as she squeezed my arm. "Well, never you mind, Kitten, we don't have to care about what Mrs. Folsom says — or thinks. We know what you *are*, and that's all that counts!"

I wanted to cry but I laughed instead. "Man, Lulu, you're really hooked. Now you're starting to sound like my grandmother!"

But Lulu didn't laugh. We both knew I was just trying to be cool about something both of us had very deep feelings about, and there was nothing else to do but turn it into a joke.

I lay on my back with my hands under my head and studied Lulu's profile as she sat and stared straight ahead of her. It was like the pictures the girls always draw when they're bored in class — a cute sort of turned-up nose and a chin that isn't too big or too small but just right. Perfect. Everything about Lulu was so perfect: her looks, her personality, her family.

"You're lucky," I blurted out before I could stop myself, "to be so perfect."

She turned and looked down at me in the queerest way. "Perfect? Kitten, what on earth do you mean?"

I shrugged, studying the clouds so I wouldn't have to look at her. "Oh, everything about you — you're so lucky. You're pretty and popular and you have this terrific family . . ."

The laugh that came out of her had no joy in it. "That's from where you sit, Kitten. Are you kidding? You're much cuter than I am. Why, I hardly have any eyebrows — at least you can't see 'em, they're so light! And my teeth are crooked and my hair — yuch!"

I really laughed now. "Oh, Lulu, stop it! You must be talking about someone else!"

She turned back and stared straight ahead again. "I wish I were. Not that looks are everything. But remember what I said before, about you, and you made fun of me? About how it's what a person is inside that counts? Well, I meant it, Kitten. You don't realize . . ." She stopped and just kept staring, and then suddenly she went on, "You know, that whole fight we had, you and me, was because of what I am inside. I lied just so I could spend some time alone with Derek. And if it'd been anyone else but you, I'd have stuck to my lie. After all I could have told you anything. I could have said that Derek lied about the whole thing to you and that everything was the way I'd told you, and you probably would never have known the difference because you'd likely as not never see Derek again to check. But there's something special about you that stopped me." She laughed that same strange laugh again. "It's funny that you're the one who got in trouble just because of that harmless little story you told that wouldn't hurt a fly. Really, I'm worse than you ever were!"

"Oh, Lulu, you're just saying that — "

"That's what you think, Kitten." Her smile had a funny twist now. "You say about my family and my being lucky. Well, I guess I am. They're good in their way, and they're nice to me mostly, and we often have lots of fun. But that's the only part you see, Kitten. You don't see our everyday selves when you come over. Lucky — ha! The only time there aren't at least two fights going on is when someone is there, and often even then, too."

I smiled. "All families have fights. You should see me and my brother!"

"You should see me and my sister. She scratches till the skin tears. That's her specialty. Mine is biting. Steve just punches. He gave Arletta a black eye once. Alfie's almost deaf in one ear from him." She looked at me now, and I guess the shock showed on my face. "You thought we're all so happy-go-lucky, didn't you? Well, sometimes we are, mostly when Daddy's working. But that's not very often. And when it is, the best part isn't that we get special presents. The best part is that he and Mama don't have as much time to fight." She turned back to her straight-ahead stare. "So you see, Kitten, I'm not all that lucky like you think. It's you that's better off. At least you have your dreams that you can escape to whenever you need to." Suddenly she turned and smiled down at me — really smiled this time. "But don't worry, Kitten, in a few years you won't need your dreams anymore. You'll have an exciting life all your own. And your grandmama and granddaddy will be there to back you up."

I sat up then. I didn't know what to say. It was all such a shock. That wonderful, warm, colorful family life the Phelpses had wasn't real at all. It was almost as unreal as my Family.

"Well, the same goes for you," was all I could think of to say. "You'll have *your* own life when you're older, too, and I guess — I guess — " I shrugged, not knowing what else to say. It was too hard to imagine such a time. We would both be so different by then.

"Oh, lots of new and wonderful things will happen to us before then," Lulu said now, suddenly brightening. "Hey, Kitten, how'd we get so serious and gloomy! Listen" — and that old sparkle lit up her face — "why don't we go on over to my house and have a little party or something this afternoon? Arletta got a new album and she's not home, so we can use it. And we can invite some other kids. There are a couple of girls around my block that seem nice. You can ask those friends of yours — what're their names?"

"Jeannie and Ann."

"Yes." She jumped up now and started dancing around. "We can have a ball, Kitten. Come on, let's ask your grandmama if it's okay."

I still sat there, just looking up at Lulu and smiling at her as if she was a little kid like Tommy or Marcy who had just done something cute. It didn't really matter at all about her family and all the things she had just told me — just like it didn't matter to her about mine. It was *us* that counted, being best friends and caring about each other and having fun together. I was lucky. I was just as lucky as Lulu. In fact, maybe I was even luckier than Lulu.

I got up, grabbing the hand she was holding out to me. "Okay, let's go ask her. It's a great idea." We started running toward the house and suddenly I stopped, pulling Lulu up short. "The best thing about the future is that it comes one day at a time."

Lulu looked at me as if I'd suddenly gone crazy. I laughed. "That's one of my grandfather's favorites. Isn't it good?"

Lulu stared at me for just another moment, and then we both burst out laughing at the same time. Our laughter grew and soon we were sitting on the ground and then rolling around with it. When we finally calmed down, we saw Grandma standing on the back porch looking at us and shaking her head as she smiled. Then her voice came to us softly. "There's nothing worth the wear of winning, but laughing and the love of friends."

She was standing in the shadows and the sun

was so bright I had to squint to see her. Like a quick, crazy flash on a TV screen, the face that smiled back at me was Mums'. I blinked and it was Grandma, all right. I knew then that she and Grandpa and Peter were all the family I had. And all I really needed.